Hush Grown People Are Talking

By LaTonya Gordon

When I was a little girl, I knew who lived in every house in my neighborhood. Before seat belts were required in the car, I used to lie down in the back seat of the car while my parents drove. I had the main street of my neighborhood memorized so well I could tell whose house I was near just by the top of the trees. I would show off by belting out family surnames as we drove past magnolias and evergreens. I felt safe and loved. I was proud to know everyone. I also know that they knew me. There was a comfort in knowing that everyone knew that I was that little " Gordon Girl" whose daddy came from "Over the river." If I ever thought of hiding or trying to get away with anything, I could forget it. I knew that if I rode my bike too fast that my Great Aunt Ruby McCall or Cousin Margaret Sims would tell my mama that I was, "In the road."

Being that the church was in my neighborhood, if I tried to eat candy or talk in church my older cousin, Oliver Sims, would tell my grandmother before I went back in the house. Back then it did not matter if it was okay to discipline other people's children. Those older folks would give one of those stern looks and everyone would get quiet. If anyone was silly enough to think of disrespecting the elderly there would be trouble. To them disrespect could come in a look, a pout, or words, and everyone would get that person straight. There were two stores in my neighborhood that were walking distance from my house. My favorite was Mr. Marion Johnson's, he ran a little green store that sat right in the middle of the neighborhood. There mothers sent their children for forgotten dry goods, children went for chocolate milk, butter cookies with a hole in the middle, and sour lemon head candies.

My house was a revolving door of teenagers visiting, or coming to stay for a while. One cousin's short stay awakened the neighborhood. I was beginning to blossom into a teenager and I wanted to follow in her footsteps. We started simply by hanging out on the porch after dark. Next it was walking to this store or that one. My parents were working and they didn't notice that I was starting to be grown. The older folks in the neighborhood noticed. One of the men told my daddy to get his shotgun ready. One older woman pulled my mother to the side and told her, "Heed my words, and take notice." She told her, "If you don't stop that child from walking the road something is going to grab hold of her and it won't turn her loose." My mother listened to that old lady and I had a hard time getting out of the house. I was known for taking short cuts and walking paths through somebody's yard, a field, or a park. With the new warning over my head if I said I was going to the store she needed a time limit and wanted to know what path I was taking. I even got the third degree if I simply said I was going for cookies. Once my mother demanded to know what kind of cookies I was going to get. My mother thought like I did, there was something about the neighborhood. People just knew things, trusted, and respected each other. We moved from house to house in the same neighborhood. Once my parents moved out of the neighborhood only to come right back to it.

Many years have passed. Most of the family is still connected to the neighborhood the ancestors lived in over a century ago. The village has lost its head leaders. Mr. Marion's store is closed, the roof is falling in. The few children that still play do it ruthlessly and there isn't anyone to stir them in the right direction. The young girls are being led astray by the older ones and there is not an older woman willing to take the young woman aside and say, "Hold onto your baby." The other men could care less about a father's shotgun. He knows that father is not in the house and waiting for the girl to become of age. There is no time for the children to get to know their neighbors because the families move in and out so much there is no need to learn to live there. The foundation of the church is still there, but older members are not the same. Now if you hushed somebody's child in church the parent may tell you off before you get off the pew. As much as the neighborhood has changed I can not see myself leaving because I still see the beauty in what it once was.

Darlington County, SC

Sweet Potato Festival

Mary Sims 1908-1940

Williams Sims
b. 1868
Darlington County, South
Carolina, USA
d. Jun 24 1925 (aged 57)
State Park, Richland County,
South Carolina, USA
m. Adelina Samuels

Adelina Samuels
b. 1871
Darlington County, South
Carolina, USA
d. Jun 05 1942 (aged 71)
Cheraw, Chesterfield County,
South Carolina, United States of
America
m. Williams Sims

Mary Sims
b. ABT 1906
Darlington County, South Carolina, USA
d. Nov 28 1940 (aged 34)
Richland, South Carolina, USA
e. Burial
Hartsville, Darlington County, South
Carolina, United States of America
e. Residence
1910
Lamar, Darlington, South Carolina
m. Isaiah W. McCall
d. Aug 29 1989
m. Ernest Hammonds
d. Oct 11 1945

Residence Notes
Age in 1910: 1; Marital Status: Single;
Relation to Head of House: Daughter

Mary Sims Part I

I never thought that I would leave my little Emma behind. I was born in a cotton country. My parents were Adelina Samuel and Cesar Sims. When I think of our family names, overall we did not go much for originality. We chose the names of aunts, uncles, and cousins. We used those names in honor and respect with the hope that those names of our ancestors carried on the good fortune for our youth. I named my child Emma, I had a sister Emma, a cousin Emma, and an aunt Emma. I'm sure that my grandmama Rena who named my aunt Emma got it from somewhere else. We borrowed from my ancestors and carried it on to our youth. Our youth carried it on to their family lines. In that way no matter how far we got we were never so far removed from each other. Although my family chose not to use my given name they called me Nonnie; Nonnie this and Nonnie that! Mind you it wasn't a bad name but, it wasn't a great one either. My life and legacy were an unwritten inheritance of sharecropping, fieldwork, or domestic work. The menfolk worked the land while the women felt they were domestics. Sometimes we were hired out in our county, neighboring counties, or towns. If we had a family member that moved to another area; that family member would speak on our behalf. There was always a family who needed *a girl*. We became those girls and we worked for those families. Unfortunately, there was an epidemic going around. Tuberculosis! It wiped out so many of our loved ones, it killed more people than were born. Generations of my family disappeared. I too succumbed to the dreaded disease. There was a point where we girls hid our illnesses. If we worked in another town, we hid who we truly were. We were just trying to survive. We wished ourselves well; we tried home remedies, and we masked our illnesses and our symptoms while keeping quiet because we knew sick folks didn't get paid.

Mary Sims Part II

I felt the need to connect with someone I've married, Ernest Hammonds. His family was from North Carolina but moved to a border town in South Carolina and lived on Railroad Ave, like Emma's birth father Isaiah McCall. That street that he lived on became Atlantic Coastline Avenue. Ernest treated Emma as if she were his child. He spoiled her and she had him wrapped around her finger. Unfortunately for my family, I worked so much now away from home, then had to work at home. After a while, I could no longer mask my symptoms and TB took over. Some of my family were shipped off to quarantined locations. I ended up at the State Park Hospital in Columbia SC. It hurt me to leave my child. I made a promise that I would see her again. I never knew that we would never see each other again. At the State Park Hospital, our living conditions were deplorable; there weren't many trained nurses. We benefited from two graduating classes of black nurses who worked in our wards. They lacked necessary supplies, were overworked, and eventually succumbed to disease as well. They wanted so desperately to change the world, to help us, but their resources were so minimal. Other folks spoke on our behalf through letters or statements. What could our saviors do for us, would they upset their lives to help us? Instead, they helped themselves because they were battling their own epidemics and they took care of their own. How dare we expect things to change?

Commissioned in 2019 by Columbia Hospital School
of Nursing Alumnae Association of Black Nurses.

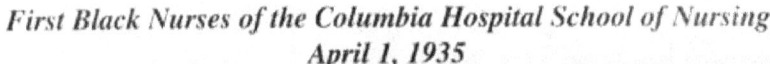
First Black Nurses of the Columbia Hospital School of Nursing
April 1, 1935

From the Columbia Hospital School of Nursing Alumnae Association

Mary Sims III

During the time I was with Isaiah, I could tell that he was a man who had a way with women. I still believed that he and I could possibly have a future here together, I was lonely here. All of my family was in Darlington County, South Carolina. There's a line in a song that says that living is easy, the fish is jumping in the cotton high. There wasn't any easy living here. Two months before my Emma was born, Mr. G.H. Turner walked out in front of a car driven by a Negro man, named Jim Walker, driving a car on Kershaw St. Witnesses said the man was speeding and didn't have lights on. Men everywhere grieved when Turner died. To them, every Negro man fit the description. There were only two words people heard, Negro man! Every negro woman working in the home of a white family was questioned. Does he own a car? Did your man drive last night? If so, where did he go? Turner's wife, Miss Flora was beside herself with worry. She was only 26 and was still trying to figure out life. She blamed every Negro man around. One month later things got worse for Negro people in the area. A robber entered the home of AG McDonald. He told everybody it was dark in the house and he could not tell if the shooter was White or Negro. All white folks seemed to hear was Negro shot a White man. It was enough for them to want revenge for every white man around.

A Tragic Accident

G. H. TURNER DIES FROM INJURIES

Cheraw Resident Struck Down by Fast-moving Auto; Driver Speeds on

George H. Turner, of Cheraw, died at the Florence Infirmary at 8:30 o'clock yesterday morning from injuries received Saturday night when he was struck down by an automobile driven by a negro whose name was given as Jim Walker. The accident occurred at the west end of Kershaw street in Cheraw as Mr. Turner was leaving his filling station. He was crossing the street, according to the report, when he was struck by a car going at a rapid rate of speed and displaying no lights.

G.H. TURNER DIES FROM INJURIES Cheraw Resident Struck Down by Put-moving Auto; Driver Speeds on H. Turner, of Cheraw, died in Florence Infirmary .11 o'clock yesterday morning injuries received Saturday night when he was struck down by an automobile driven by a negro whose- name was given as Walker. The accident occurred at the west end of Kershaw Cheraw as Mr. Turner was leaving his filling station. A tragic accident such as this one would have been talked about by most of the residents in the small town.

Mary Sims IV

During my hospital time, I spent my days and nights praying. I thanked God for the time I was able to spend with my daughter and for the family that she had loving and helping her get through these days without me. I didn't understand why our lives had taken this path, why so many people were affected by the deadly disease. We tried to be careful and clean to kill germs as best we could. We cleaned and disinfected where we worked, and with the ones we loved, to keep them well. We failed!

I lay in that bed and I watched death court patients. Death wooed the ill with hope. They had sweaty fever kisses. A death rattle hummed a lullaby in their chest and orgasmic moments of in and out of consciousness. The final moments were spent spooning in an embrace with the grim reaper. We knew that death would never stand up to us, or duel for us with another lover. Death was a horrible faithful lover.

> In 1934, the typical patient admitted to the sanatorium was a young woman in her late teens or early 20's with far advanced pulmonary tuberculosis. In addition to the basic treatment of bed rest, collapse measures were directed toward the lung disease. There were 15,000 active tuberculosis cases in the state and an average of three persons died daily, most of whom died at home because of the dearth of sanatorium beds.

Mary Sims Death Certificate

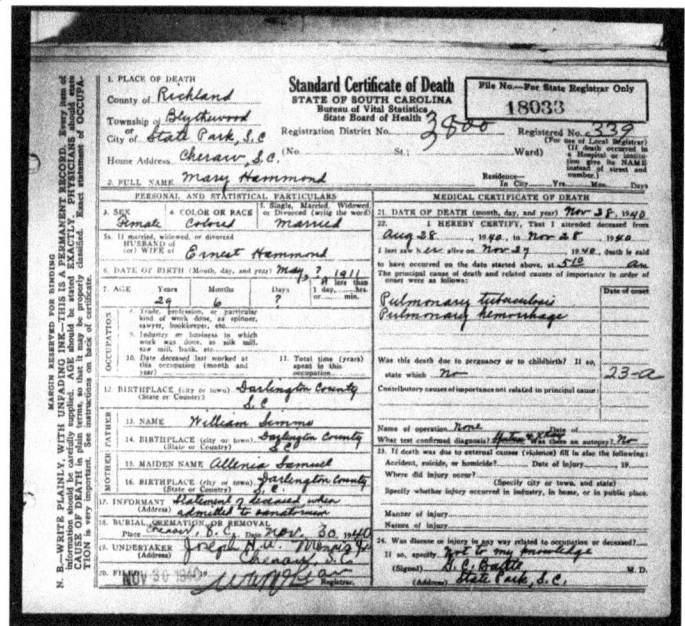

Mary Sims Hammond, daughter of Adlena Samuel and William Sims, died in a State Run Facility. She, like many others of their time, suffered greatly from Tuberculosis.

Palmetto Hall was one of the several places around the country that served black patients who were quarantined from tuberculosis and other contagions.

(Abandoned Southeast, 2021)

Lucy Bostick Sims circa 1820

The cotton fields are talking, slaves are telling each other about the plantation business, while they pick the cotton in the fields. Master Daniel Dubose is taking ill and is writing his will. Tom and I are going to be given to his son-in-law. Slaves in the house are saying that all babies born to me belong to him. It is terrible that my body and my children aren't even mine.

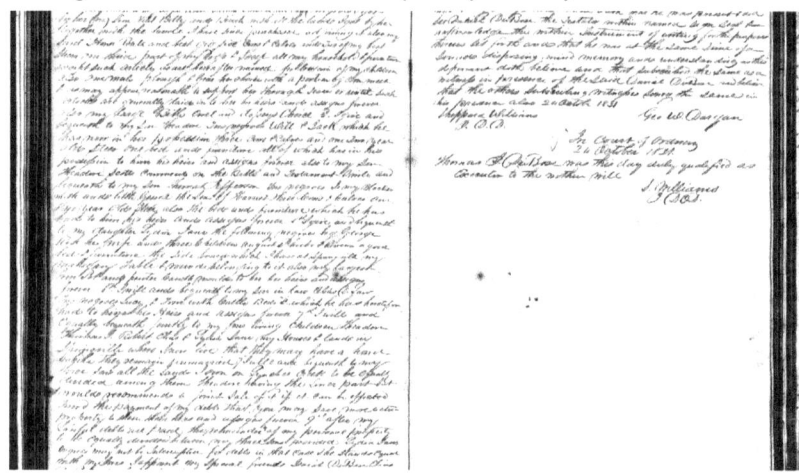

Image of the will of Daniel Dubose

Transcribed Record of Lucy Bostic Sims

Name	Lucy
Relationship	Enslaved Person
Item Description	Will Book, Vol 8-10, 1829-1859

Individuals Listed (Name)	Relationship
Daniel Dubose	
Thomas Jefferson	Son
Lydia Jane	Daughter
Auguste	Child
Phoebe	Child
Romena	Child
Elias D. Law	Son-in-law
Lucy	**Enslaved Person**
Tom	Enslaved Person
Theodore	Child
Thomas I.	Child
Robert Elias	Child
Lydia Jane	Child
Isaiah Dubose	Friend
Elias D. Law	Friend
Thomas I. Dubose	Friend

Margaret Sims Moore I circa 1912

Most of the family has moved up north. I get a call or a letter from everyone once in a while to let me know how they're doing. I've never birthed a child but my hands have raised many. I tried my best to let them feel that I was there for them. I gave them the best of what I had. This house came to us through Oliver's teachings, his books from Eastside School are still in the room. My mama Minnie's sweaters are boxed up in the attic. Rosalie's little whatnots are still on the table. The children I raised are all gone with families of their own. There are no faces to wash or clothes to dry. All that is left are empty rooms where life used to be. Some days I take a little sip or taste and they will help me forget the loneliness that they left behind. I spent my days washing clothes and laundry at the Holly Inn Motel where I used to work. Now I watch people pass from my front porch or window. There life happens, here I just sit and watch time pass.

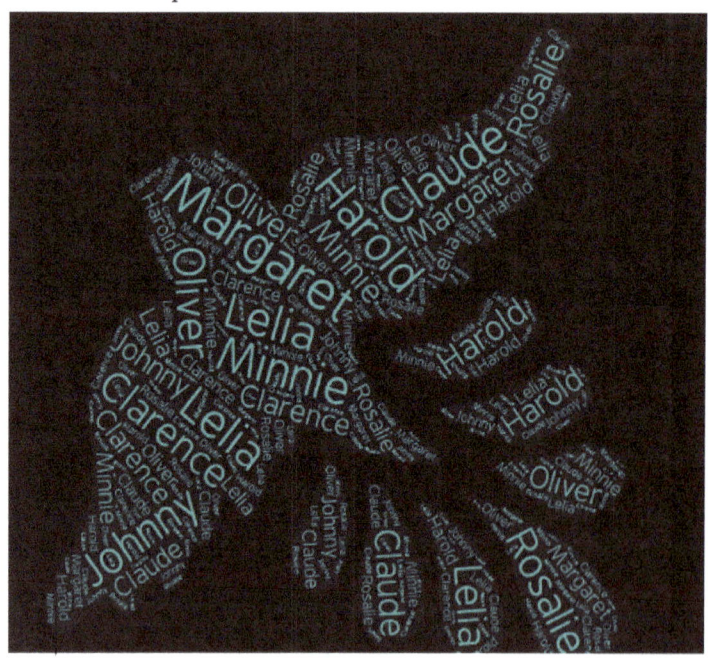

Minnie Sims and Latonya Gordon

Rosalee Sims

Margaret Sims Moore II

I have just finished doing the last of the laundry for the Holly Inn Hotel. Ms. Adelaid Marshall has an out of town guest coming in from New York. She says they are old friends of hers from her Cotton Club days. I noticed she has been singing a little more around here. Her fancy friends will come into town talking like big shots. It won't last long, they never do. My mama always said that people like that won't ever let any grass grow under their feet and they have to keep moving. I think she just misses her old dancing days.

COTTON CLUB DANCER

Adelaide Marshall

	Adelaide Marshall
e	Female
dor	Single
rital Status	23
ge	abt 1914
Birth Date	South Carolina
Birth Place	Cheraw
Other Birth Place	Le Havre, France
Departure Port	14 Jan 1937
Arrival Date	New York, New
Arrival Port	Paris
Ship Name	

BEAUTY AND CHARM OF 1938

Mother Of Cotton Club Immortal Buried Here

By ALLAN W. McMILLAN

Mrs. Inez Talley Marshall, mother of the famous Cotton Club beaut Adelaide Marshall, was buried in pomp and glory here last Wednesday afternoon at Woodlawn cemetery. Mrs. Marshall died of a heart attack at her home, 24 Hemingway ave., New Rochelle, on Saturday morning, Oct. 1. She was 67 years old.

BELOVED BY CELEBS

Mrs. Marshall was born in Cheraw, S.C., the daughter of the late Winslow and Isabelle Tally. She lived there until her marriage to the late Edward Marshall. The family moved to New York city in 1929 with their two daughters, Adelaide and Thelma. Adelaide later became the toast of the Cotton Club as one of its show girls.

At the rosary service held at Jenkins Funeral home Tuesday night, hundreds of personalities from theaters and night clubs

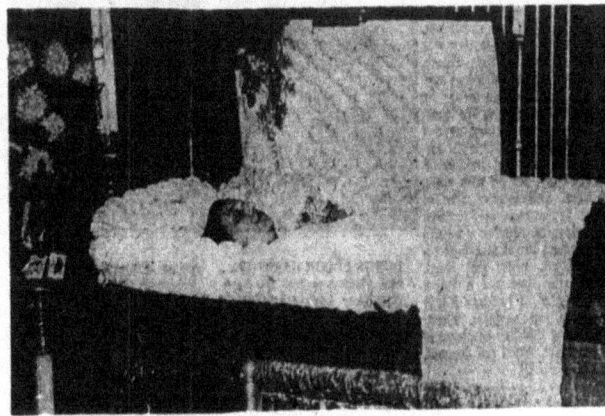

MRS. INEZ MARSHALL

"Adelaide Marshall The" Cotton Club"

ALLOTMENT ANNIES are operating full-blast just like in WORLD WAR II. The poor soldiers who marry those chicks on such short notice should have their heads examined. One ANNIE has a 'husband' at QUANTICO; another in TOKIO and a third in BERLIN . . . ADELAIDE MARSHALL is just as spry as she used to be during her COTTON CLUB days. Her versions of the CHARLESTON and BLACK BOTTOM are out of this world . . . LLOYD GIBSON says he doesn't bother with that girl anymore because she is too much for him . . . UNION JOE hasn't let any grass grow under his feet since his wife cut out. He is now more than friendly with a new chick who calls herself the 'housekeeper' . . . Loan sharks are cutting each other's throats trying to get most of the heavy sugar in bailing out prostitutes.

The most vital community service performed by DEPUTY INSPECTOR EDWARD G. McGLONE during his tour of duty as Commanding Officer of the 28th Precinct on West 123rd Street was the revocation of hundreds of gun permits issued to irresponsible characters. His successor, CAPTAIN JAMES J. BOLAND

Allotment Annies were women who married soldiers during WWI.

Willie Mae Sims circa 1917

Also known as Mama Sweet

My daughter Sally has come home to visit from New York. I fixed her a big plate of my old country cooking. I know she misses my food and can't get the same taste there. After she finished eating, she and I went outside and started talking, trying to catch up. My neighbor, Nancy McCormick came over and we let life breeze by laughing and talking. Every once in a while Sally would yell, "There goes another one." We would look up and see someone walking in the railroad ditch over the tracks trying to get on the other side of the street. One of these days these men walking through that ditch may fall down in it. I hope I never see the day that happens.

Willie Mae Sims
"Mama Sweet"

Sally Johnson

LaTonya Gordon with Sally Johnson

My daddy is standing in the yard talking to our neighbor over his homemade pallet fence. They are marveling about how my daddy squeezed his little Chevy Chevette between the fence and the magnolia tree. My mother is standing by her Buick Mercury with her hands on her hips. Her expression says we need to leave now! My brother and I are in the back seat and he keeps hitting my arm . Our destination is our cousin Sally's house. My younger brother reached the steps of the house before the rest of us. We are barely inside when he finds a group of children to play with. I glanced around for any teenagers my age, there aren't any. Sally and her sweetheart, Mr. Brown, talk loudly on the sofa amongst other adults around the room. My parents find their place easily on loveseats. I sit at the bar in the kitchen and I am served koolaid in a green ribbed glass. I'm trying to ease my boredom and I get an eerie feeling. It seems that the adults are waiting for something. My brother and another child were running about the room. I was certain they would be punished, instead Sally just laughed and gave them more sweets. She's his godmother and thinks everything he does is fine. I was engrossed in watching the young kids play and looking around the room. A quiet hull fell over the room and the adults seemed anxious. The front door swings open and a skinny black man pounces in the room with a Santa Claus Suit. He laughs and shouts, "Ho Ho Ho." The children in the room comes running to him telling him about their Christmas wishes. My brother hesitates back for a moment. His face has a distorted grin, he sniffs loudly and says, "Santa Claus smells like beer." Everyone laughs, and I shake my head. This was the first time I ever met a skinny drunk Santa.

Oliver Sims Part 1

People are spreading rumors again! I'm just trying to live my life! They always ask where my wife is. Why did I never get married? Did I ever want children? I've overheard them saying something is wrong with the man living alone. I teach children every day and I see what they become. I watched most of my family die of tuberculosis, and it almost took me. My cousins and I were all spread out everywhere after our parents died. Why would I want another family that could die to leave me too? I'm just trying to teach. It is hard for a colored teacher in this world. The school district does not give colored schools up to date materials. My Eastside high students are learning from my materials. They need to let me do it while I can. Everyone wants me to live differently. I just want to live in peace.

❖ Oliver Caesar Sims stooping down at a Homecoming Church Service at New Hopewell Baptist Church, in Darlington County SC.

❖ Oliver Sims is featured in the photo. The photo is sponsored by the
   Marlboro County School Community Center

❖ East Side Elementary and High School opened in 1954 as the black
   school in Bennettsville, SC. After integration, the school became an
   elementary school.

History credited to Rebekah Dobrasko

STATE OF SOUTH CAROLINA	)	LAST WILL AND TESTAMENT
	)	OF
COUNTY OF CHESTERFIELD	)	OLIVER CAESAR SIMS

I, Oliver Caesar Sims, a resident of and domiciled in the City of Cheraw, in the State and County aforesaid, do hereby make, publish and declare this to be my Last Will and Testament, hereby revoking all Wills and Codicils at any time heretofore made by me.

ITEM I

I do hereby direct my Co-Personal Representatives hereinafter named to hold a Christian service at the Pee Dee Union Baptist Church within forty-eight hours or as soon thereafter as may be practical following the time of my death. I direct that there be a casket spray but no other flowers or floral arrangements except two fresh green arrangements and also that no obituary be published by newspaper, circular or radio. I further direct that at the said service the minister shall read the twenty-seventh chapter of the Book of Psalms of the King James Version of the Holy Bible. I direct that the only music shall be live music with no recorded music allowed. I further direct that only family members can view my body after it is embalmed and that I then want my casket sealed and no one further allowed to view my body.

ITEM II

I direct that my Co-Personal Representatives pay my funeral and other just debts as soon after my death as may be practical.

ITEM III

I do hereby devise and bequeath my house and lot located at 2 Martin Luther King Drive, Cheraw, South Carolina, as well as that vacant lot of land

30

Oliver Sims part II

Emma just left my home with her grandchildren. She's trying to get everything right for her grandchildren's school. She grieved heavily for her daughter-in-law Lola. She still speaks highly of her and how she asked her to watch over her children. She is a woman of her word and will make sure those children will be taken care of. I give my advice when I can, especially when it comes to school. I stopped teaching for quite some time but I told her I'd help her with the schoolwork if they needed it. I see my help does not stop at school work. I have to extend that help to church too. As soon as Emma's uncle Robert McCall starts playing the music, and she marches in with the choir those children get to giggling and laughing. They know that Emma didn't raise them like that.

❖ Oliver was noted to be a stern educator, and very opinionated in family affairs, giving unsolicited advice.

Annie Cornelia Cosom part I

Daddy can't allow himself to look in our eyes. He blames himself because he couldn't help Mama. She was sent away to get help, he thought doing so was best for her. He never imagined those would be the last moments he saw her. Mama was taken away and placed in an institution. Some official-looking white man came to the house and said Mama had expired. I found out later that expired meant that she passed away. They gave Daddy a piece of paper that said she died from shock. She had only been gone for two days, now no one would ever see her again. Anybody who knew my Mama, Janie Sims Cosom, knew she wasn't scared of anything. If she could survive cotton country in Dovesville, South Carolina surely, she could survive anything.

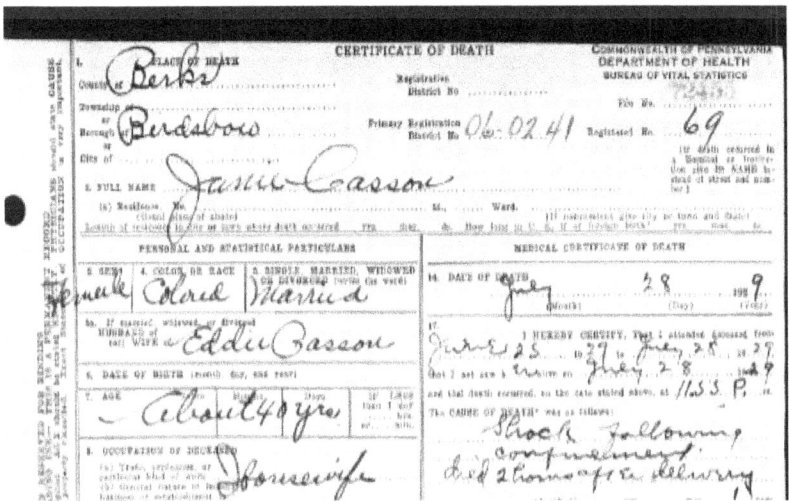

❖ Southerner, Janie Sims Cosom, died two hours after being confined in a Pennsylvanian institution.

Annie Cornelia Cosom part II

The weather is really cold here. I've been doing my best to make sure Jerome has what he needs. I worked a lot of our jobs. I know that he's a grown man now with a family of his own but I still worry about my child. So every day I work at this station. One ticket at a time I plan my future.

ANNIE
CORNEILA
COSOM

Loving. Sweet.
Dedicated

This photo shows a retired Annie Corneila Cosom. After several years of working in New York, she returned down south to live and chose to worship at her family's home church, New Hopewell Baptist Church, Hartville

New Hopewell Baptist Church, Hartsville SC

(New Hopewell Baptist Church 2022 courtesy of Facebook

Annie Cornelia Cosom Part III

My God daughters Tonya and Renee are standing on the historic Morris College campus in Sumter, South Carolina. They were raised in different counties and went to different high schools. Who knew they would end up in the same college, in the same year, and in the same dorm? They are getting along well and have become fast friends. I hope they continue to stay close. Finding new friends isn't always easy, especially

after you have moved away from home. I'm glad they have each other.

Historic Record

LARGE NUMBER OF STUDENTS AT OPENING

Record 'Attendance at Morris College, Colored School

BEGINS 17TH SESSION

Ministers of the City and County Speak at Opening Exercises

Morris College began its 17th session Wednesday, September 24. On account of the heavy rains many were prevented from being at chapel Wednesday morning.

91 CITED FOR ACADEMIC HONORS

Ninety-one students who excelled academically at Morris College during the 1997 spring semester were recognized Thursday at the annual Honors Day Convocation.

The program, held in the Neal-Jones Auditorium, featured an address by Dr. Mary Vereen-Gordon, Morris' academic dean.

Honorees included four students on the President's List with perfect 4.0 grade point averages: freshman Vakenya L. Brunson, biology major; sophomore Emily O'Neil, English major; juniors Leonard O. Griffin and Sadie F. Jeter, pastoral ministry majors.

Also receiving special recognition were three scholars who have been named to the President's List and/or dean's list for six consecutive semesters: Mahassen Banks, junior English major; Latonya Gordon, senior English major; and KaDana Simmons, senior biology major.

Twenty-three students were named to the dean's list with 3.4 to 3.9 grade point averages: seniors Felicia D. Collier, Willis C. Cooper, Jamey Graham and Roeethyll Lunn; juniors Carolyn M. Dyson, Eric B. Green, Caroline Johnson, Marcia L. Pack, Christopher D. Scotland, Larry Swinton, Charlene J. Williams, Renete' N. Williams, and McKaren D. Williamson; sophomores Chandra Benjamin, Melissa N. Boykin, Theresa A. Cousar, Quinton L. McClary, Raymond L. Perdue, and Melissa R. Richardson; freshmen Debra Bennett, Veronica A. Jefferson, Kaamel A. Leonard and Jacquel M. Thomas.

*The author is noted in the clipping

Emma McCall Part I

These days are uneasy and have not been for a while. My mama left me early in life and has been gone for five years. She raised me as best she could and married well to my stepfather, Ernest Hammond. I just got word that he has just been shot in the chest and died. My first born baby is only a month old. My stepfather barely got to see him. He wasn't happy that I was going to have a baby so young. He started to feel better about everything once I married Willie. He wanted well for me, and I hate that he won't see what good things I will do. Something doesn't sit right with all of this surrounding his death. Ms. Flossie Davis is the one who let everyone know that he passed. I wonder if she knows more, but is afraid to get involved.

Emma McCall Part II

Willie and I have driven with the kids to Lancaster for Camp Meeting. I'm struggling to keep up with all the children and he is running around grinning and smiling in all the women's faces. I know that he still has some family left up here, but he isn't talking to them. His first wife, Louise, warned me that he was like that. I didn't listen to her. He is over there eating food from different women. There is one particular one he keeps looking at. This Thompson girl had some fried chicken and greens out here, There is no way she could have kept that food from turning out here. She doesn't look all that clean. I wouldn't eat that food with a borrowed mouth. When his stomach gets to hurting I'm not going to unseal my lips to help him.

❖ Though this story is completely fictional, the family had a history of attending Camp Meeting in Lancaster SC.

❖ The first wife and second wife were friendly to each other, they are pictured posing in a cotton field.

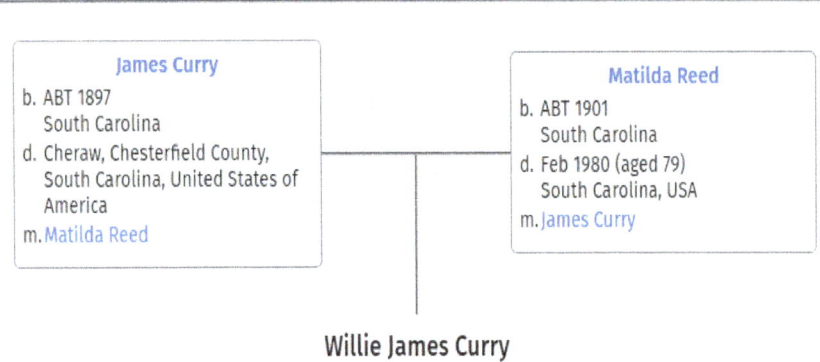

James Curry
b. ABT 1897
   South Carolina
d. Cheraw, Chesterfield County,
   South Carolina, United States of
   America
m. Matilda Reed

Matilda Reed
b. ABT 1901
   South Carolina
d. Feb 1980 (aged 79)
   South Carolina, USA
m. James Curry

Willie James Curry

The ladies pose in a cotton field after a trip out of town for lunch.

Pictured here are Rosa Lee Sims, Louise Haggard, Dorthy Curry Robinson, Emma McCall Curry and Willie Sims Johnson

Mount Carmel A.M.E. Zion Church & Campground is a historic African Methodist Episcopal Zion located in Heath Spring, a county in Lancaster South Carolina was founded by former slave, Isom C Clinton. He served as bishop, treasurer, and property owner.

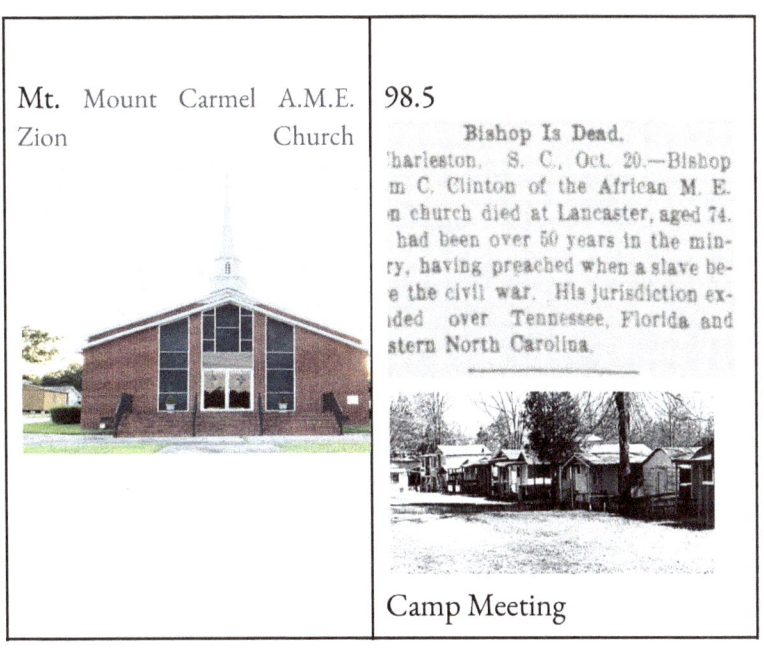

Mt. Mount Carmel A.M.E. Zion Church

98.5

Bishop Is Dead.

harleston, S. C., Oct. 20.—Bishop m C. Clinton of the African M. E. n church died at Lancaster, aged 74. had been over 50 years in the min- ry, having preached when a slave be- e the civil war. His jurisdiction ex- ided over Tennessee, Florida and stern North Carolina.

Camp Meeting

Mt. Carmel Historical Marker

Emma McCall Part III

Miss Matilda just left this house with Willie's older children. She is lugging those teenagers around, and they don't want to be bothered. She is one mean woman, and nothing I do is good enough for her. Lord is this what I get for marrying a yellow man with a yellow mama? His first wife, Lousie, warned me not to marry him. I should have listened.

❖ Many blended families struggle to maintain healthy relationships, however, in this family line, the first and second wives developed friendships and were cordial to each other.

❖ 1950 census records have Matilda's grandchildren living in the home with her. In later years they often visited Emma and their siblings.

Household members

Name	Age
James Curry	58
Matilda Curry	56
Dorothy Curry	16
Willie J Curry	15
Frances Curry	7
Thomas F Curry	12

Matilda Reid Part I

1894-1980

My son, Willie, has just left here with his new wife, Emma. She came in holding her baby, and that is not Willie's child. He's too dark to be his child, and if he has any more with Emma, there's no telling what color the other children will turn out.   We've always taught my children to lighten up the family line. Willie has brought home a dark skinned girl. He knew better, and their lives will not be easy.

- ❖ My late grandmother shared an event of meeting her mother-in-law for the first time and the issues she had experienced with colorism.
- ❖ Colorism has transcended generations and cultures around the world. It impacts class status, education and employment.

> WANTED FOR COLORED CAFE AT 1114 Washington. 4 neat looking light colored girls. Salary $8 per week. meals free, 8 hrs. work daily. Apply all day Thursday.

The advertisement is for a black-owned business seeking only light-complexioned women. SC-The State Newspaper 1942.

Isaac Barnes

b. ABT 1854
   South Carolina

m. Matilda Short

Matilda Short

b. ABT 1857
   South Carolina

m. Isaac Barnes

Hester Barnes

b. Feb 1877
   , South Carolina, United States

d. Cane Creek, Lancaster, South Carolina,
   USA

e. Residence
   1880
   Cedar Creek, Lancaster, South Carolina,
   USA
   Marital Status: Single; Relation to Head:
   Daughter

m. Peter Reid
   1891

Peter Reid

b. Apr 1876
   South Carolina

d. Cane Creek, Lancaster, South
   Carolina, USA

m. Hester Barnes

Hester Barnes

b. Feb 1877
   , South Carolina, United States

d. Cane Creek, Lancaster, South
   Carolina, USA

m. Peter Reid

Matilda Reed

b. ABT 1901
   South Carolina

d. Feb 1980 (aged 79)
   South Carolina, USA

e. Residence
   1900
   Cane Creek, Lancaster, South Carolina,
   USA
   Marital Status: Single; Relation to Head:
   Daughter

m. James Curry

Matilda Reid and Mother Hester Barnes circa

The Barnes, Reids, and Currys were a tri-racial group of African American, Caucasian, and Native American. It is possible they descended from enslavers, and one of the Cherokee, the Catawba, or the Waxhaw tribes that existed in the area. (History of Lancaster)

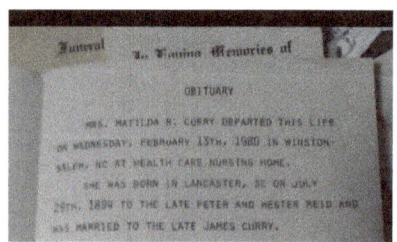

Matilda Reid Part II

Willie said they named the baby Chalmers after my brother. He was a barber, an intelligent family man. That's a family name, and at least the name will carry on. It is an honor to be named after a loved one. She seems to be a good mother. Things may go well for them.

Matilda Reid Part III

My brother Chalmers, whom we call Buddy, has passed on. I took on his girls Mary Hester, and Sammie Lee to care for. Now they are grown up and doing well. Mary Hester has joined the army and married a man named Bogan in New Orleans. His family is from Mississippi deeper south thank we are. Down there black people are not loved by all people like they should.

Emma McCall IV

My father Isaiah McCall, "Zell" as I like to call him, has married a woman from the low country down near Charleston. Most people call those people from that area Gullah Geechee. He met her at her father's church while he was singing in Uncle Robert's choir. She came from a very large family. He married such a young woman. I guess if they have any children my children will be older than theirs.

Emma McCall with her father Isiah McCall.

EMMA MCCALL

Activist

Headstrong
Fierce
Dependable
Suvivor

Emma McCall Part V

It's time for Barbara Lawrence School to open back up. My girls have sent their children there. One of my older grandchildren graduated a few years ago from there and went on to primary school. The others are just getting started this school year.The children are coming from all over Cheraw, Chesterfield, and across the river in the Sandhills. They look right cute with their little lunch boxes going to school. When the grandchildren get home they talk about the different colors they are learning. The count is as high as possible. and sing a lot of different songs. One of the songs they sing is about picking up Paw Paw and putting it in the basket. One day I'll ask the teachers about what Paw Paw is. Their moms have spent many times picking cotton or hearing about the trials of picking cotton. It is funny to sing about times like that. I'm glad the school is there and they get to learn from people who live here, work here, and worship here. At the primary school, where my other granddaughter went, the teachers won't look like us or worship where we do. My uncle Cesar Sims is now going to be taught by the director of the school, Mrs.Bernice Robinson.

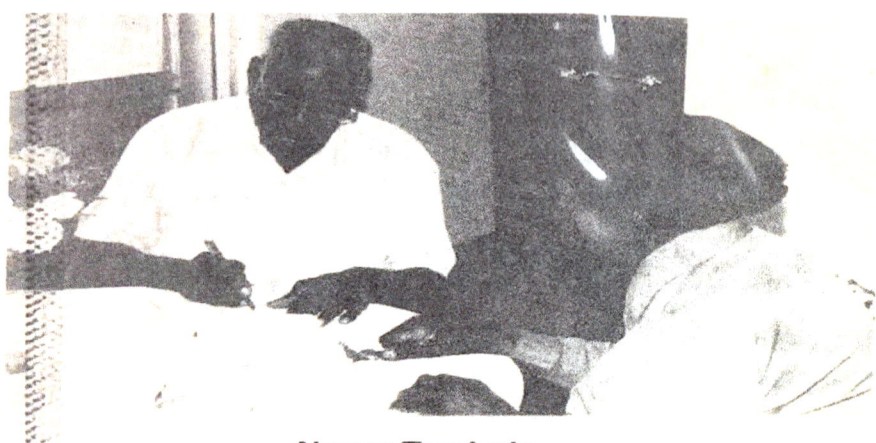

Never Too Late

Ceaser Sim proves it is never too late to learn. For the first time in his 69 years, he can write his name, and the names of his immediate relatives. In addition, he can read the Level I Lauback reading materials. Also shown is Bernice Robinson, a volunteer tutor who has taught Mr. Sims. Others can become involved by accepting help from a volunteer tutor or volunteering as a tutor. Call the Chesterfield County School District at 623-2175. This service is provided to the county by the Chesterfield County School District Reading Campaign. (Staff Photo)

❖ Mrs. Bernice Robinson retired counselor and educator for forty-one years at Chesterfield County School District, and fifteen years as a director at Barbara Lawrence School.

Cesar Sims and Latonya Gordon

Barbara Lawrence School

Pictures courtesy Matheson Library Donated Historical Records
Teachers: Mrs. Geneva Thomas and Ms. Carrie McIntosh
The School Barabra Lawerence

Emma McCall VI

It is New Year's Eve, and for the first time in years I have all of my children home. I will gather them around to pray before the New Year comes. Earlier today I sent the girls out to order groceries from Winn Dixie. I need to make sure all my generations get blessed with those black eyes peas and collard greens. Those peas stand for the coins and the collard greens stand for the money. I'll be praying for wealth over all of our lives. The ones that live up north stopped on their way down on Interstate 95 and got fireworks. I can't stand to hear all of that, but I won't say anything. I'm just glad to have them home. The children are playing free tag by the tree out front. Some of them are grilling a whole hog out back, I heard my back door opening and closing. They know I don't like anybody going through my back door, anything may crawl in. I won't say about that, but I will stop all of my grands from running in and out of the house, wallowing on my beds, and washing their hands in my kitchen sink. They better go down to the bathroom sink for that.

Railroad Town
Cheraw, SC

SCL (ACL) STA. CHERAW, S. C.   NOV. 1973

This photograph is from the Railroads Photograph Collection, Folder 10926 1-40,
Accession number 10926-20 housed at South Caroliniana Library

George Walton McCall

Robert Lewis McCall	Son	1916 - 2003
Jeanette E McCall	Daughter	1900 - 1955
George McCall	Son	1904 - 1941
Sarah McCall	Daughter	1909 - ????
Margaret Louise McCall	Daughter	1913 - ????
Edmund Mccall	Son	1917 - 1932
Minnie McCall	Daughter	1894 - 1936
Mere McCall	Son	1918 - 1918
Ruby Ellen McCall	Daughter	1893 - 1989
Hattie McCall Blue	Daughter	1894 - 1922
Evans McCall	Son	1899 - 1974
Ellen Alia McCall	Son	
Henry McCall	Son	
Georgia B Rountree	Daughter	1914 - 1998
Amelia McCall	Daughter	1918 - 1918

Ruby McCall Wilson
1895-1989

When people tell their stories of their life and how they came to be they always start with the beginnings. They would talk about their surroundings and all of the ancestors who spoke of their existence and prayed over their lives. When they tell their life stories of their time in between those moments of their life sometimes they tell what's familiar, what's easy, what's happy. They don't want to always tell the sad or the unjust things that they did. So I'll share a little bit of mine. I had a daughter named Willie. She carried the name of her grandfather. She was a happy girl; she and her cousin Anna Wright would spend days laughing and talking late into the night, like most girls her age. She was lovely! She works hard like most for her age trying her best to please her parents, but I kept a secret from the world. When my daughter was sixteen, she was with a child, and she suffered trying to bring that child to life. For two days I watched her fight for her life, fight for the life of her child. It broke my heart that I vowed never to speak her name again. Even after her death, my name is not listed on her death certificate. It just says the name of her father, my husband and it doesn't even list his last name. "Ranson's girl" are two words that sums up her existence: I lost my daughter and my grandchild. I lost what was mine, what would have been mine. So today I honor her and I tell the story of Willie Wilson, the daughter of Ruby Ellen McCall and Ranson Wilson. Our beautiful happy daughter now may rest in peace. I did have the pleasure of raising another child. My brother Isaiah had twin sons, he kept one and I kept the other one. I raised him as my own; he was my boy! I love him, and I love his children. Hopefully, they kept fond memories of me. There were times when I kissed his little face, or offered words of encouragement in my distant memories when I thought about my girl. I wondered if she were alive and what she would be doing now. I wondered if I did the right things by her or if I did enough in her life. I even wonder if I should have told her story today. Her death certificate says Ranson's girl, but she wasn't just his, she was also mine.

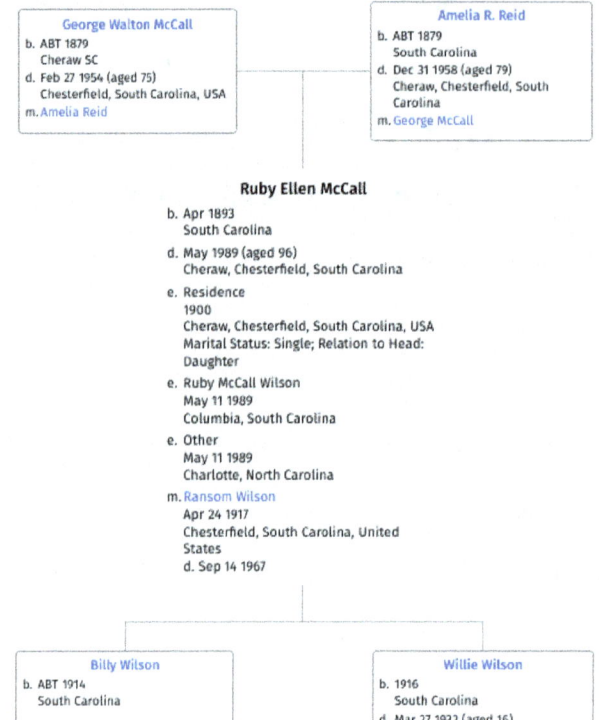

George Walton McCall
b. ABT 1879
  Cheraw SC
d. Feb 27 1954 (aged 75)
  Chesterfield, South Carolina, USA
m. Amelia Reid

Amelia R. Reid
b. ABT 1879
  South Carolina
d. Dec 31 1958 (aged 79)
  Cheraw, Chesterfield, South
  Carolina
m. George McCall

Ruby Ellen McCall
b. Apr 1893
  South Carolina
d. May 1989 (aged 96)
  Cheraw, Chesterfield, South Carolina
e. Residence
  1900
  Cheraw, Chesterfield, South Carolina, USA
  Marital Status: Single; Relation to Head:
  Daughter
e. Ruby McCall Wilson
  May 11 1989
  Columbia, South Carolina
e. Other
  May 11 1989
  Charlotte, North Carolina
m. Ransom Wilson
  Apr 24 1917
  Chesterfield, South Carolina, United
  States
  d. Sep 14 1967

Billy Wilson
b. ABT 1914
  South Carolina

Willie Wilson
b. 1916
  South Carolina
d. Mar 27 1932 (aged 16)
  Chesterfield, South Carolina, USA

Name	**Willie Wilson**
Birth Year	abt 1915
Gender	Female
Race	Negro (Black)
Age in 1930	15
Birthplace	South Carolina
Marital Status	Single
Relation to Head of House	Daughter
Home in 1930	Cheraw, Chesterfield, South Carolina, USA
Map of Home	Cheraw,Chesterfield,South Carolina
Street Address	Industrial Section
Ward of City	3
House Number	405
Dwelling Number	244
Family Number	250
Attended School	Yes
Able to Read and Write	Yes
Father's Birthplace	South Carolina
Mother's Birthplace	South Carolina
Able to Speak English	Yes
Neighbors	View others on page

Household members

Name	Age
Ransom Wilson	33
Ruby Wilson	31
Willie Wilson	15
Anna M Wright	15

Mrs. Ruby M. Wilson

CHERAW

Mrs. Ruby Ellen McCall Wilson, widow of Ransom Wilson, died Sunday.

Born in Chesterfield County, she was a daughter of the late George and Amelia Reid McColl. She was a member of Pee Dee Union Baptist Church, the senior choir and pastor's aid committee. She was a deaconess, missionary, head of the arts and craft department of the Pee Dee Association and an officer of the Pee Dee Women's District convention. She received state awards from the Grand Chapter of the Order of the Eastern Star and was a Past Matron of Venus Chapter No. 51.

Amanda Shields McCall

John Evans and his sweet wife Nellie invited me to have dinner with them last night. Poor thing barely had time to cook. She had just gotten in from teaching at the school and John Evans came home not long after that. He brought one of his lawyer friends from Bennettsville and they were talking about a big case with Early Funderburk. I hope they win the case. It will be good for the community. Some officials had the two of them on a board to represent the negroes to ease the integration process. Some of the blacks around here are scared that they are stirring up trouble with the NAACP. It got out they went down to Orangeburg for a meeting with other Negro lawyers and the people are scared they will bring back trouble. We all ought to glad somebody willing to stand up and fight for the negro race.

Attorney John E. McCall

Flemming-McCall, F. (2008) McCall, Spencer Group photo (2023

Court Cases

Betterson v. Stewart

245 S.C. 296 (1965)

140 S.E.2d 482

S. E. BETTERSON, Marshall Brantley and Joseph Orr, Individually, and as Electors, Taxpayers, and Parents of Negro School Pupils of Jasper County High and Elementary Schools, and on behalf of themselves and all others similarly situated, Appellants, v. Paul Allen STEWART, Individually and as Supervising Principal teacher of Area No. 1, Jasper County Negro High and Elementary Echools, Respondent.

18300 Supreme Court of South Carolina.

February 9, 1965.

*297 Messrs. Frank E. Cain, Jr., of Bennettsville, John H. Wrighten, of Charleston, and John E. McCall, of Cheraw, for Appellants.

Messrs. Luke N. Brown, Jr., and Walker & McKellar, of Ridgeland, for Respondent.

State v. Funderburke

251 S.C. 536 (1968)

164 S.E.2d 309

The STATE, Respondent, v. Early FUNDERBURKE, Appellant.

18842 Supreme Court of South Carolina.

November 19, 1968.

*537 Messrs. John E. McCall, of Cheraw, and Frank E. Cain, Jr., of Bennettsville, for Appellant.

*538 Messrs. Marion H. Kinton, Solicitor, of Dillon and J. Dupre Miller, Assistant Solicitor, of Bennettsville, for Respondent.

Ruth Love McCall

Robert has gathered all of those people up to go to Charlotte to appear on TV. I hardly get to see him between his teaching at the colored school, working on the radio station and going on the air at 6:00 in the morning. Now he is making that album and they will appear on television. I'm not even sure if I know all of those people and if they can all sing. Yet here he is practicing and getting mad if they are singing off-key. I've been trying to get him to sit down long enough to eat, but he is in here bouncing around talking about how he has to go.

Community loses musical pioneer in car accident

By LEIGHTON BELL
and WYLIE COX
Staff Writers

An elderly man died last Thursday in a car accident on West Market Street in Cheraw. Robert Lewis McCall, a lifelong resident of Cheraw and highly recognized member of the African-American community, was pronounced dead on the scene, according to Lance Corporal Bryan McDougald of the South Carolina Highway Patrol.

The accident occurred around 7 p.m. Feb. 27 when McCall pulled his Chevy Lumina out in front of an oncoming Ford Explorer travelling on West Market Street, according to the police report. The driver of the Explorer, Sammie J. Garris, 28, of 5455 Hunts Mill Road in Chesterfield, along with her 9-year-old passenger, were both

transported to Chesterfield General Hospital. They were treated for minor injuries and released the same night of the accident.

McDougald said all three people involved in the accident were wearing their seatbelts.

McCall of 130 Harrell St.

was the last surviving child of George and Amelia McCall of Cheraw. A member of Pee Dee Union Baptist Church, he attended Coulter Academy, Benedict College and Morris College and earned a bachelor's in elementary education. He taught school in Chesterfield, Great Falls and

Marion and was principal of a small school in Patrick before desegregation.

His real passion in life was music, according to family members. He began his musical studies with Alice Wilson of Cheraw, who was also an early instructor of Dizzy Gillespie. McCall first played at the Pee Dee Union Baptist Church of Cheraw where his musical and choirmaster skills quickly became legendary. As the family recalled, a member of the congregation once remarked to a young McCall, "Hey boy, you get notes out of that organ them other fellows didn't know was in there!" From then on he willingly lent his talents to the service of his community, playing at weddings, funerals and church functions for people of all races and walks of life.

SEE McCALL, PAGE 7A

Photo courtesy of the McCall family
The musical skills of Robert McCall, who passed away last week, were legendary at his church, Pee Dee Union Baptist Church.

McCall was also the first black radio announcer in the Cheraw area. He was on air with WBSC out of Bennettsville.

The Cheraw Chronicle 2003

Robert L. McCall founded and directed several choirs. The McCall Singers was a traveling choir.   He directed the album for " The Nation's Most Renowned Pee Dee Choral Ensemble, Cheraw, South Carolina"   Those who performed on the album were the following: Geneva Thomas, Ophelia Ellerbe, Roosevelt Bradley, Henry McCall, Robert McCall, Daniel Hughes, vocals.

The Nation's Most Renowned

PEE DEE CHORAL ENSEMBLE

Cheraw, South Carolina

Album Cover Courtesy of Baylor University

INTERESTING NOTES ABOUT THIS
FINE CHOIR

The Pee Dee Choral Ensemble was
founded in the year of 1945 from the church
edifice of the Great Pee Dee Baptist Church
where James C. Levy Sr. is Minister in Cheraw, South Carolina.

This Choir has seldom reached the
peak that is found in this most stirring album. As these songs are sung by these
well trained voices one can almost feel and
communicate with our Lord and Savior.
The feeling of the spirit and love from on
high penetrates through excellent blend
which makes this choir one of the nation's
most renowned. For years this Choir tour-
ed many towns and cities, appearing and
performing before the most thrilled, appre-
ciative, and enthused audiences. It took
it's place with radio, concert, and television
appearances. We style this album as a
replica of God's word and the only addition
is the tender melodic interpetation of the
Pee Dee Choral Ensemble as directed by
Robert Lewis McCall, Assistant Director,
Roosevelt Bradley; President, James Ellerbe Sr.; and Secretary, Carrie Hughes. The
soloist are Geneva Thomas, Ophelia Ellerbe, Roosevelt Bradley, Henry McCall, Robert McCall, and Daniel Hughes.

THE NATION'S MOST RENOWNED
PEC DEE CHORAL ENSEMBLE

SIDE I

1. Get Right With God
2. Every Step of the Way
3. Roll Jordan Roll
4. Won't It Be Greed
5. Trying to Get Ready
6. I've Got A Home In That Rock

SIDE II

1. Leaning on the Everlasting Arms
2. I'll Go Lord
3. I Want To be Ready
4. Windstorm and There's Going
   To Be A Meeting

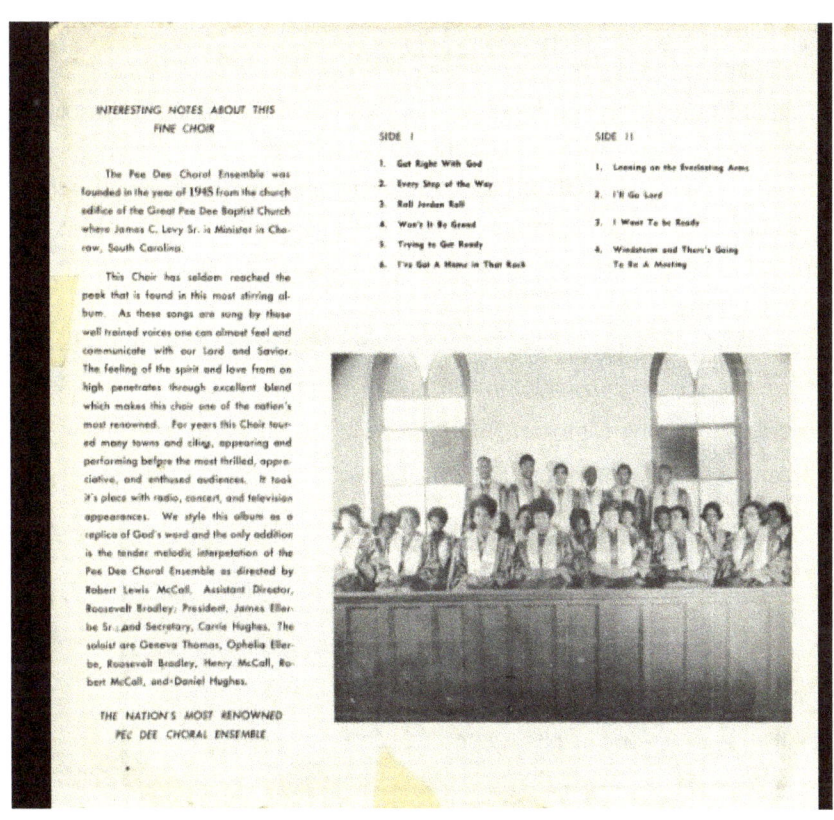

Album Cover Courtesy of Baylor University

Sarah Ellen Holmes McCall Circa 1850

Adaline Pegues from Anson and I got to talking about our children and husbands. I got to talking about my husband and my son Israel and how he was so good at figuring numbers. She got to talking about her son Albert and how he is preaching so young and going to school to teach. I hated to tell her that all negros do is farm, teach or preach. Her boy has now done them all. It seems that all of those folks up this way are so uppity.

❖ Sarah McCall may not have known Adaline Pegues or ever communicated with her. They both had connections in Cheraw, SC. Sarah's son Israel became a merchant grocer. Adaline's son was educated in Cheraw and became a prominent minister and professor.

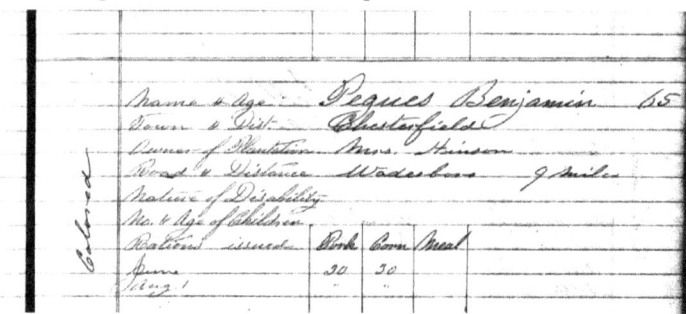

❖ Benjamin Pegues listed on the Freedman's bureau on the Hinson Plantation

Dr. Albert Pegues, Negro Educator, Dies At Raleigh

Raleigh, July 28.—(AP)—Dr. Albert W. Pegues, dean of the theological department of Shaw university, corresponding secretary of the negro Baptist Sunday school convention and for 40 years leader among the negro Baptists of the state, died at his home, 125 East South street, today at 4 p. m.

Dr. Pegeus was in his 70th year. He was born in McFarland, S. C., November 25, 1859. The funeral service will take place here Wednesday afternoon.

Mary Bell McCall Rogers

Most of my family has moved up here from Railroad Avenue in Chesterfield County South Carolina. My mama remarried after my daddy Israel died. I know that it was difficult for her to continue caring at the grocery store. It's not easy for a colored woman to live down south unaccompanied by a man. Most likely my brothers will work in the steel industry up here, like my brother Israel. My dearest friend is Mary Edwards who was born in Society Hill but moved to Cheraw. She and her husband live on my street. We have many days of talking and laughing. Our neighborhood is full of people from Greece, Italy, and Romania. Her friendly face helps me muddle through so I won't lose myself in all of these people. My little Anna plays with her little Norman. She is a little bossy like he is her toy being that she is three years older. He is just happy to have a friend.

❖ It took several years to learn anything about Mary Belle, The life of her family was cut short due to health reasons. Her daughter, Anna, spent over four years in a Sanitorium due to tuberculosis.

Frances McCall circa 1877

The twins Daniel and Timmy have been very active lately. I try to keep them as busy as I can, but having two at the same time they have always been the go. They fall in line with the other children.

Birthplace	South Carolina
Home in 1920	Cheraw, Chesterfield, South Carolina
Street	Rail Road Ave
Residence Date	1920
Race	Black
Gender	Male
Relation to Head of House	Son
Marital Status	Single
Father's Name	Thomas Hughes
Father's Birthplace	South Carolina
Mother's Name	Frances Hughes
Mother's Birthplace	South Carolina
Attended School	yes
Neighbors	View others on page

Household members

Name	Age
Thomas Hughes	50
Frances Hughes	40
Pauline Hughes	23
Tom Hughes	21
Mattie Hughes	20
David Hughes	13
Timmy Garnal Hughes	8
Danl Hughes	8
Paul Hughes	4

❖ Daniel and Timothy Hughes were the first set of twins noted coming from the McCall line by their mother Francis McCall Hughes

❖ Francis' brother Henry McCall Swinney there are eight sets of twins (noted in family reunion video archives)

❖ Francis' nephew Isaiah W McCall there are eight sets of twins (the author knows them all

❖ Francis' nephew Nelson McCall there are four sets of twins (this fact is noted by Mr. Spencer E. McCall family historian and genealogist)

❖ Florence, South Carolina • Sun, Nov 21, 1971 research does not note if the families above are related or not.

(STAFF PHOTO BY JOHNNY ELLIS)

MR. AND MRS. ROBERT McCALL, LEFT, AND MR. AND MRS. JAMES McCALL DISPLAY THEIR TWINS
The McCall Brothers Married Sisters and the Sisters Gave Birth to Twins the Same Week

For a Couple of Florence Couples Everything Seems to Come in Pairs

By LESLIE TROUT
Morning News Staff Writer

Mr. and Mrs. Robert McCall and Mr. and Mrs. James McCall have a lot more in common than their last name.

It was usual enough when the two couples were married, because James and Robert are brothers and their wives, Sophia and Mary Ellen, are sisters.

But, the situation was made more unique last month, when both Mrs. McCalls had twin boys during the same week.

Both sets of twins were delivered at McLeod Memorial Hospital by the same doctor, who informed Mrs. James McCall and Mrs. Robert McCall that they each had given birth to sets of identical twins. Mrs. James McCall noted that having identical twins is by itself quite unusual.

"I was just shocked," said Mrs. James McCall. She pointed out that she did not know she was to become the mother of twins until after she had given birth Oct. 18.

Mrs. Robert McCall's twin boys were born Oct. 7. The Robert McCall's already had a set of five-year old twin girls and a four-year-old daughter.

"I'm telling you, its a whole lot of work — double work," Mrs. Robert McCall said, adding, "I wouldn't trade these two for anything." She said her husband and children are delighted, and she "can't keep them away from the babies."

Robert McCall said Mrs. Annie Belle Williams, the maternal grandmother of the "double first cousins," was "thrilled" when she heard the news. Mrs. Williams had only one grandson and was pleased to find her daughters had given birth to four more so soon.

Refusing to "take the blame" completely for the birth of the twins, the McCall ladies were quick to add that "twins run in the McCall family."

Both families reside in the 1200 block of Dixie Street and attend the Church of God. James McCall and Robert McCall are also employed by the same company, Vulcraft Division of the Nuclear Corp. of American.

Robert McCall said he's been kidded a lot at work since his second set of twins was born. He said his friends are always asking "what my secret is" and "why I couldn't just stop at one."

All four of the baby boys have similar names. The children of Mr. and Mrs. James McCall are named Sherwin and Ronald Stefon. Mr. and Mrs. Robert McCall named their babies Robert Sherman and Roswell Sherlock.

The mothers said they expect to dress their children alike and hope they will have a chance to grow up more like quadruplets than "two sets of twins."

Mrs. Robert McCall said both couples met at church and "sort of grew up together." Mr. and Mrs. Robert McCall were married in 1965. He is 31 and his wife is 30.

James and Sophia McCall have been married less than a year. Mrs. James McCall pointed out that she had to give birth to twins, "just to keep up with my sister." James McCall is 36 and his wife is 25.

As far as having any more children goes, Mrs. Robert McCall hopes "this is it," while her sister isn't planning to increase the size of her family, "for a while, anyway."

Elizabeth Ellerbe Hughes

It is hard to go back to the church and know my sweet Frances won't be there singing in the choir. The whole congregation is hurt, I try not to question God. I try not to judge my child, or Dr. Hanna's son. People whisper, but they are respectful enough to offer condolences, food, and wipes my tears. I won't get to see her beautiful smile, hear her laughter or her soulful songs on the radio with her sister on piano or with young Ted Bradley in their duets. He called them the spiritual twins, such a sweet nickname for them. What happens when there is only one left?

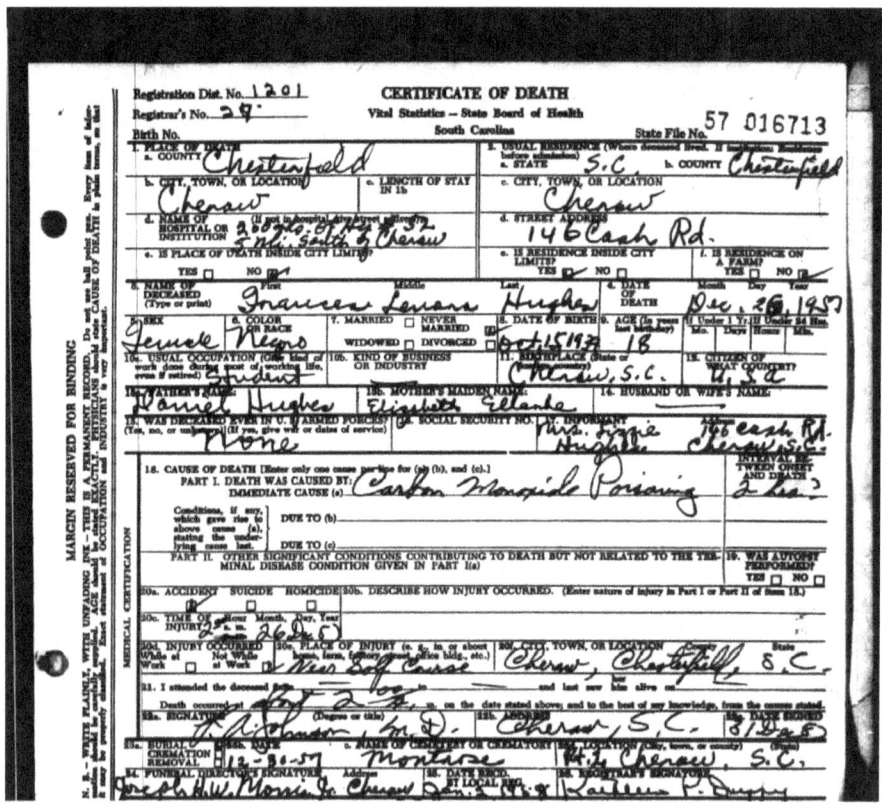

George McCall
1904-1941

Ruth and I had a time getting the saints to settle down at Pee Dee Union today. I was tired from my job as a Porter on the railroad. The members were angry with Louis Easterling. He started a fire to burn off his land. The fire caught a hold of one of his little buildings he had some furniture in. He had some kind of insurance on it. The saints said that nothing in the building was worth anything and that he was trying to collect some money off it. If the church had burned they would have never let him see the light of day. They are still in mourning after the tornado took the first one down. I bet that foolish man. He won't try that again. It is one thing to fool the insurance people, it is another thing to mess with the saint's place of worship. Cousin Claudius would give up northern life and move back south.

Fire Sunday morning about 3 o'clock destroyed a small building over on "river hill" just to the rear of the colored Baptist church. The building was beyond the water limits. Louis Easterling, colored, had a lot of furniture stored in the building, on which we understand he had some insurance. The building and contents were a total loss.

●●●

Pee Dee Union Baptist Church has a rich history starting from 1867 with London Windsom, followed by Claudius McCall.

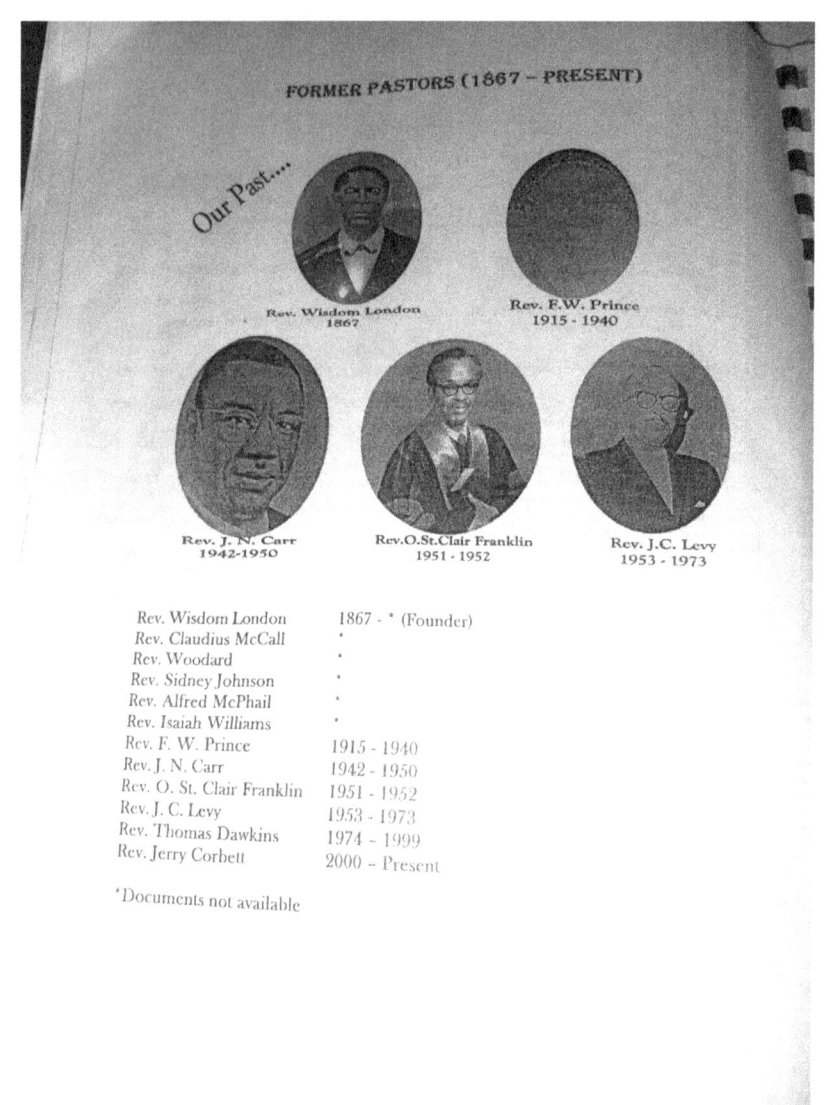

FORMER PASTORS (1867 – PRESENT)

Our Past....

Rev. Wisdom London
1867

Rev. F.W. Prince
1915 - 1940

Rev. J. N. Carr
1942-1950

Rev.O.St.Clair Franklin
1951 - 1952

Rev. J.C. Levy
1953 - 1973

Rev. Wisdom London	1867 - * (Founder)
Rev. Claudius McCall	*
Rev. Woodard	*
Rev. Sidney Johnson	*
Rev. Alfred McPhail	*
Rev. Isaiah Williams	*
Rev. F. W. Prince	1915 - 1940
Rev. J. N. Carr	1942 - 1950
Rev. O. St. Clair Franklin	1951 - 1952
Rev. J. C. Levy	1953 - 1973
Rev. Thomas Dawkins	1974 - 1999
Rev. Jerry Corbett	2000 – Present

*Documents not available

This fact was taken from Pee Dee Union Baptist Church History

Founding Pastors of Pee Dee Union Baptist Church

London

McCall

Latonya Gordon with John Highland III

Today my mama shuffled my little brother and I in her brown station wagon. She drove to Howard street to pick up a family friend, Mr. John Highland. He is the oldest person I have ever known, being that he is almost one hundred years old. His mind is sharp, and he can get around very well. Unfortunately he is hard of hearing. Last week we took him with us while we shopped out of town. He was in the store talking about people. He thought he was whispering but they could hear him. I was embarrassed, my mom did not seem to mind because she was too busy keeping up with my brother who was touching everything in the store. When I got back to the house Mr. Highland gave my brother a statue of a ceramic dog. He did what every little boy would do, pretended the dog was real. I sat on his long plastic covered sofa. He let me practice dialing on his rotary phone. My fingers never seemed to get it right. He and my mama were talking about his bicycle. I never thought anyone that age would still ride a bicycle.

❖ Mr. Highland lived to be 104 years old. He was living on his own for some time. The local newspaper, The Cheraw Chronicle, wrote a feature story about his life and photographed him riding the bicycle.

Title	Page 1
State	Delaware
Full Name	Highland, John
Birth Place	South Carolina
Birth Date	29 Apr 1890
Race	Colored
Residence	Wilmington, New Castle, Delaware
Conflict Period	World War I
Served For	United States of America
Views	1

CHERAW — Mr. John W. Highland III, 104, retired Pee Dee Union Baptist Church custodian, died Oct. 9, 1994, at Cheraw Health Care. Funeral is 1 p.m. Saturday at Pee Dee Union Baptist Church. Reid's is in charge.

Survivors are his son, Johnnie Highland of Columbia; daughter, Mrs. Lola Fletcher of Washington; grandchildren.

Cheraw, S. C.

By LEVI G. BYRD

Mr. and Mrs. John Highland of Howard Street, attended the graduation exercises of their daughter, Millie, from St. Agnes School of Nursing in Raleigh, N. C. Among others attending were Mrs. Hubert Austin, Mrs. Garthree Short, Mrs. Nelson McQueen and D. Duncan.

Latonya Gordon with D.D Duncan

Everybody is excited, we are headed to Carowinds. This is my mama's third trip full of kids on a journey. In October my mama had Mr. Duncan drive us to the state fair, in May we went to Myrtle Beach and this June we are going to Carowinds. She spent all night frying chicken and making sandwiches. She said some mamas send their children with just enough money to ride the bus and she has to make sure everybody has enough to eat. Five cars dropped off children to the house to spend the night last night. My daddy said the trips were fine but the kids could come by in the morning without having to be dropped off the night before.He would grumble and complain but he couldn't help joking around making everyone laugh with his antics. My mama always loved having the laughter of children around. This time my daddy decided to stay out of the way and got busy taking out his strobe light from his blue station wagon. Yesterday his former coworkers and friends from Pyramid Screen Printing told him he needed to take those things off of his car because he would get in trouble. My daddy liked the element of surprise and would flash those lights as if a police car were coming up on people. My mama shook her head and was going back and forth from the house peeking at my daddy trying to get him to help load the last items on the bus. Mr. Duncan was already in the driver's seat waiting patiently. I climbed on the bus with my cousin giggling as we went. I asked him the same questions I always did: how far is it, and is it going to take a long time? He looked at me and smiled and answered like he was never bothered. The noise of teenagers and adolescence never got on his nerves and he drove year after year. He was a lot like my mama and he had a kind heart for the youth.

- ❖ Mr. Duncan was active at Pee Dee Union Baptist Church; he had careers in trucking, insurance sales, and, in later years driving buses.
- ❖ He and his teacher wife, Cleo, were part of the affluent families in Cheraw.

Quicktown

Willis Turlington. Full report next week.

ROUTE DISCONTINUED.

The mail route to Dargan, Quick and Kollock from Bennettsville, which has been in operation for some time, has been discontinued and the offices at each. Our subscribers at Quick can get their papers changed to either Cheraw or Bennettsville.

Bennettsville, South Carolina • Fri, Apr 25, 1890 Page 5

Dick Quick circa 1810

Master Thomas Quick over here in the Marlboro District needs me to make more shoes for the horses. I was low on materials so he is sending my sons James, and Silas and I over the Horace King bridge to Cheraw to get more. Miss Aquilla has been really angry because the horses aren't up to her standards. No matter what I do I can't do things right for them.

HORACE KING

HORACE KING BORN
CHERAW, SC 1824

1. ARCHITECT
2. ENGINEER
3.CONSTRUCTOR

❖ Enslaved Dick Quick is listed in the of Thomas Quick in the Marlboro District of SC along with two other slaves Amelia and her son Moses.

Another story of the remarkable length to which human life extends is told by The Pee Dee Advocate. This instance of longevity is, as frequently transpires, that of a negro slave, and unlike most such cases it is claimed that records of her age have been preserved. The Advocate says:

"Last week Harriett Quick, the oldest person living in Marlboro county, died at her home in North Smithville. She was 114 years of age and this was really her age as the records have been preserved. She was a colored woman, and was a slave owned by old man Bennie Quick, who bought her from a northern speculator who brought her direct from Africa. She raised a large family and had by actual count 245 children, grand and great-grandchildren. She was industrious, after the war saved her annual earnings, and purchased 500 acres of land all of which she absolutely owned at the time of her death. She was buried at Ebenezer (old Quick's) church, in the presence of a large assembly of both white and colored."

Silas Quick
b. ABT 1830
    Marlboro County, South Carolina,
    USA
d. , Marlboro, South Carolina,
    United States
m. Mary Quick

Mary Quick
b. ABT 1862
    South Carolina
d. , Marlboro, South Carolina,
    United States
m. Silas Quick

Mary Ann Quick
b. ABT 1857
    South Carolina, USA
d. Jan 10 1948 (aged 91)
    Hamlet Route 2, Richmond, North Carolina
e. Residence
    1870
    Hebron, Marlboro, South Carolina, USA
    Post Office: Bennettsville
m. Quick UNKNOWN
m. Madison Bright
m. Andrew Easterling
    1882

Mary Ann Quick circa 1857

I, a woman of mixed heritage, didn't really fit any mold. I did not fit in with the darker-skinned blacks, and I most certainly didn't fit in with white people. Most black people assumed that I had a higher advantage because I was of a lighter complexion. Many whites assumed that I was being uppity. I do have to admit I fared a little better than the average black woman during my time, but I like so many others had my struggles too. However, I had the good fortune of bringing into the world a daughter a beautiful girl named Delia, Carrie Delia.   Many people wonder about her parentage. They wondered about her father only my closest friends knew of him, and I won't even tell you. Her early days were good, I married well, and we got for her all that our money could afford.   When I was growing up I always had a slew of family and friends to play with. Most were all neighbors' children and family members. Many were Quicks, of course, being that was my last name. The surnames of some of the other families were Chavis, Odoms, and Jacobs. I played with Black, White, and Indian children. We call them Indian then it was okay to do so back then but I didn't go around announcing this is my white cousin, this is my Indian cousin, this my black cousin in that community we blended as one.

Some of the best parts of living in the country of the Carolinas are between one and three o'clock each day in all four seasons. In the summer, after I've had the hottest part of my day. The clouds start to darken. The muggy thick air cools. Thunder rumbles in the distance, and sharp flashes of lightning remind me that God is still in control. In the spring I watch the slight shift of the leaves on the trees. The smell of rain before it falls is the promise of God's kisses upon my head, no need to water the garden tonight. In the fall of the year, I grab my straw broom and I sweep the yard of leaves. Just when my arms start to tire, I complain that I worked harder than I intended to work. I admire my hard work, turn to go inside and two single leaves fall reminding me that God is not finished with me yet. When old man winter comes singing the blues, and my aching bones can't stand another minute; I get caught up in one spot where the sun shines. In that moment it is as God says I will always give you what you need.

Andrew Easterling circa 1844

Mary Ann has been down all week. She lost her kinfolk, James Preston Quick. It is the oddest thing, people are saying he took his life. People are saying he went down to the store and got some laudraum. That isn't like him, he was always happy! He joked around with his sisters and brothers and is always sweet on his wife. It doesn't make sense! I just don't believe it, and neither can Mary Ann, with them being so agreeable with each other every time they saw each other. The older folks are talking about his soul and how he won't make it to Heaven. I think something happened to him. If he did it, he must have been mad in the head. We have got to find some answers or the rest of who are still

living will never find any peace.

- ❖ Laudaum- was used as a medicine to aid people before others realized it was used to end their lives. Here is an example in 1907 ad in Goldsboro, NC.

- ❖ There is no guarantee that Mary Ann Quick and James Preston Quick were related, but they lived in the same community, same surname, and during the same time period.

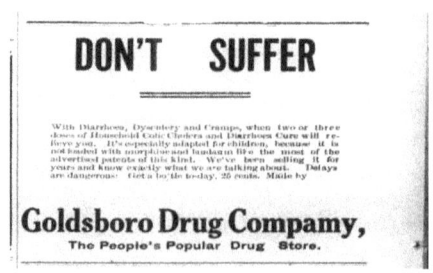

march 14, 1906.

A STRANGE SUICIDE.

Takes Laudanum and Lays Down On the Railroad Track.

James Preston Quick, a well known colored citizen of Smithville, was found dead on the Seaboard Railroad Tuesday morning about 8 o'clock by the section crew near Mr. Zack T. Pearson's Fruit Farm. During Monday evening he went to Mr. Pearson's store and purchased a bottle of Laudanum, He asked the clerk if there was directions on the bottle. The clerk replied that there was. Quick then asked how much would it take to kill a man. The clerk thought he was just joking. He then left the store about 8 o'clock and went off towards the Railroad. It was supposed that he drank the Laudanum and then lay down on the track with his head across the rail with his body parallel with the cross ties and fell asleep. He was struck by a passing train, which crushed the back part of his head

It is said that entanglement of his business affairs lead him to this act. He was a clever, good farmer, running five plows, and he passed for a pious quiet citizen.

He was about 34 years old and leaves a wife, mother, six brothers and five sisters.

Aggie Quick circa 1830

Little Maria Odom from down the road has come in the hot June night worried about her mama. She came frantic and in tears yelling about the baby coming and something is wrong. My daughter Emmeline calmed her down while I got my bag. I marched down the road as fast as I could just in case the girl wasn't hysterical for nothing. The first thing I did was pray, the second thing I did was put a penny under the mattress for blessing and protection. One look at Maria I could tell the baby was breech and I had work to do. I have caught many babies, and helped many mothers, this one won't be any different. One day she will tell her story of how her little one tried to come feet first ready for the world.

Name	**Aggie Quick**
Age	50
Birth Date	Abt 1830
Birthplace	South Carolina
Home in 1880	Brightsville, Marlboro, South Carolina, USA
Dwelling Number	311
Race	Mulatto
Gender	Female
Relation to Head of House	Self (Head)
Marital Status	Widowed
Father's Birthplace	South Carolina
Mother's Birthplace	South Carolina
Occupation	Midwife
Cannot Read	Y
Cannot Write	Y

❖ My third great grandmother Aggie Quick and Maria Odom were neighbors. In June of 1880 she had a one year old son William. It is quite possible that Aggie was the midwife who delivered her baby.

Quick-Fair Women

Carrie D   Carrie P   Betty A   Edna B

Hamlet, NC

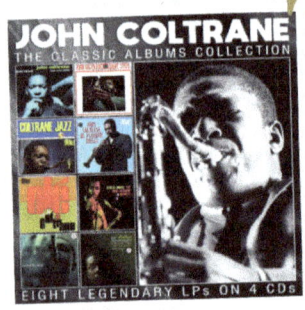

Carrie Delia Fair I

John Wellington has started to lose his eyesight. I try to keep him encouraged and talk about good things to him. It is hard to see a good man go downhill. My grandchildren have been coming around to help me out around the house and to keep him company. My daughter Bernice Clinton comes down with her children every once in a while. It is good that she lives close by. One thing I can say about family is that we always lean on each other.

Carrie Delia Fair Part II

I'm worried for my Alonza. he is married to Tessa Locklear. She comes from a wild family mixture of Locklears and Quicks. They are black, white, indian. Some of her family still lived on the Indian reservation, the plantation, blacks in the sandhills and whites in hiding. She doesn't know who she is or who she wants to be and she takes it out on my son. I pray his days are happy ones.

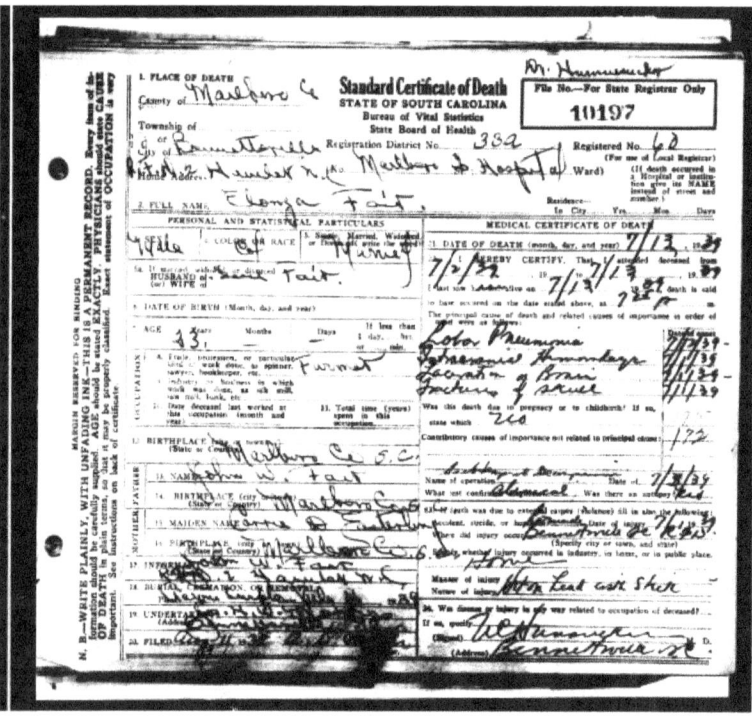

Alonza was hit in the head by his wife while he was ill, no charges were filed. Tessa's Quick line were founders of the historic church Aaron's Temple named after her grandfather who was sold away in slavery. Her grandmother Harriet named the church after her husband and she lived from 1789-1903. The family line connects again with the marriage Alonza's uncle James B. Easterling to Daisey Quick.

Tessa Locklear's cousin Reverend Harrison Ingram Quick became a prominent minister, landowner, landlord, and Justice of the peace. He was a feature in a book <u>History of the American Negro and his Institutions</u> by Arthur B. Caldwell.

HARRISON INGRAM QUICK

LaTonya Gordon with Hazel Fair

Today my mama and daddy and I are in our blue station wagon. We are in a procession of cars following each other. It is Christmas time and the family members are going caroling. I have always seen people on TV doing Christmas carols. Today we are those people! We stopped at Great Aunt Hazel's house. She lives near the Dobbins Heights area in Hamlet, NC. She is my grandmother's older sister. When she opened the door and saw all of her nieces and nephews she hollered with joy. She started hugging everyone and told us all to come inside. Once we were there she listened to the family sing Christmas songs. My favorite song was "Jingle Bells" because my cousins from Bennettsville sang another version and changed the lyrics to, "Jingle Bells, Batman smells and Robin laid an egg." My daddy's oldest sister told them to stop that. They laughed and whispered it when the adults went back to talking. Aunt Hazel brought out a chocolate with pecans on top. She gave us really huge slices. I decided right then that chocolate was my favorite. I hope we come back to visit.

❖ I shared this memory with a family member. They said she was known for baking and that her cakes were really good.

Kollock, Marlboro SC

BENNETTSVILLE & CHERAW • Kollock, South Carolina • John Krause

Willie Mae Joseph

My husband Maynard has got the news that his mama Katie Delia Harrington has passed on from a stroke. I know he is a little down right now, but thankfully he has his faith in the Lord to keep him going. I know that the funeral will be very big with all the family. It will be full of his side with the Kollocks, Boatwrights, and Harringtons. My family of Quicks, and Easterlings will be there too. With all our family there people will be inside and outside of Ebenezer Church just to support each other. It doesn't matter that it will be crowded. The family is there to show love and that is what love does.

❖ Ebenzer United Methodist Church history notes that Maynard started in ministry in 1951.

The Harringtons

Maynard and Willie Mae

Julia Kollock circa 1862

Mama and daddy say the census man has said we need to have a last name. They have chosen to go with Gordon after our grandfather Rueben who was sold away and sent west. When I was a little girl they said we were Kollocks based on grandfather Jack. I won't be part of that. If we have to choose a name then I will choose for myself. My brother Jacob is fine with the name change, not me! My Freedom means having the right to do as I please. And I will choose the name I want at least for a little while. I will be married soon, and carry the name of my husband. My name is all I have to call my own.

Name	Julia Kollock
Age in 1870	8
Birth Date	abt 1862
Birthplace	South Carolina
Dwelling Number	195
Home in 1870	Smithville, Marlboro, South Carolina
Race	Black
Gender	Female
Post Office	Bennettsville
Occupation	At Home

In the 1880 census all of the family members were together as Gordon except Julia. The only other record of Julia is from her brother Jacob who noted that he lived with her and her husband.

Railford Dumas "Grandpa Sip) circa 1839

Photo courtesy of descendant Lillie Christian from Gordon Family Collection

Hattie Dumas Part 1 Jacob's First Wife

Jacob has been gone for some time. The doors always open from these drafting nights. I keep hoping when it opens it'll be him coming back to us. Jimmy has become a hard boy. There isn't any joy in him now. Ludie stays close to home and visits his grandmother Louisa from time to time. Their relationship is something special. I'm glad to see that he still has joy and love and carries it. Their grandfather Alexander has provided what he could to help and had left word of what has happened with Jacob. None of that matters, he's not here, and like most women I have to make do.

❖ There are not many records of Hattie/Harriet other than the fact that she is the mother of James "Jimmy" Gordon and William Ludie Gordon.

Ganey, Hazel; Goings, Pate; Gordon, William; Gordon, James; Hinson, James F.; Hinson, Ben; House, C. Harmon; Howell, Alexander; Horton, Gib; Hull, Lonnie; Ingram, James; Jackson, Lovelace; Jackson, Melton; Jackson, Luther; Jackson, Freeman; Jackson, Ben; James, Alex; Johnson, Sailor; Johnson, Dolhpus; King, Patrick.

Lane, J. Jasper; Lane, John L.

❖ James Gordon and William Ludie Gordon are registered to vote in a 1917 election.

James "Jimmy" Gordon & William Ludie Gordon

James "Jimmy" Presley Gordon

I got a letter today that little Sadie Ellis is getting married to a man named Johnny Martin. It seems like yesterday she was a little girl. I looked back at the picture of her and Annie Lee Larrant. She is sitting down looking so focused. I hope she will have a blessed union and that her life will be a good one.

Name	Johnnie Marvin Martin
Sex	**Male**
Age	**32**
Birth Year (Estimated)	**1910**
Race	**Colored**
Spouse's Name	**Sadie Vivian Ellis**
Spouse's Sex	**Female**
Spouse's Age	**29**
Spouse's Birth Year (Estimated)	**1913**
Spouse's Race	**Colored**
Event Type	**Marriage License**
Event Date	**28 Mar 1942**
Event Place	**Marlboro, South Carolina, United States**
Event Place (Original)	**Marlboro, South Carolina**

Rebecca Ellison

Tonight I watched Ludie stand on the floor holding his head. there were no words, he didn't need to say anything. His grandmother, Lousia Harrington, was gone. He had just come in to let the people know she passed. They wrote it down that he was an informant. He made a habit of going by her house every day, to check on her and Mr. Ciserio. When she couldn't take care of herself anymore, he brought her home to us. I watched this strong man grieve his grandma. He was there when she closed her eyes. This is one of those moments when you still thank God for knowing her. Grandma Louisa caught our baby Sam. She was a midwife, and the first hand to hold our child. My husband Ludie, was the last one to hold hers.

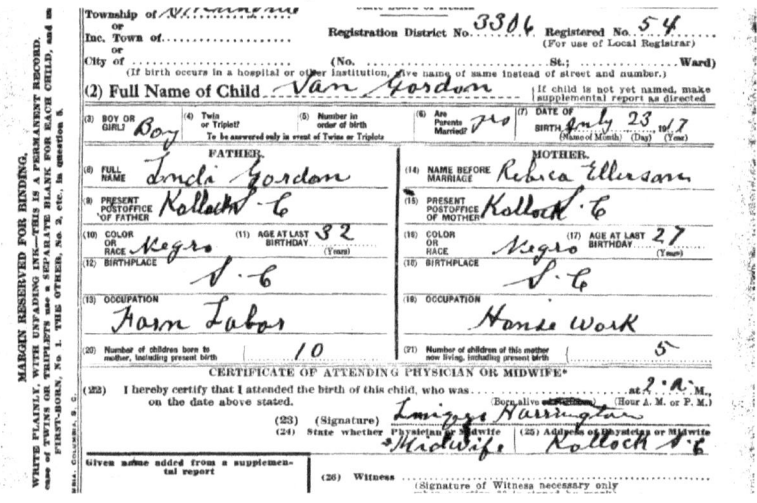

Twenty-three days after the loss of Mrs. Louisa Harrington her husband passed away. There is a saying in the southern community that when two loved ones pass away in a small window of time the last person dies from a broken heart.

Alexander Gordon circa 1840

A free negro, Hugh Clark, has asked for Mr. Charles T. McRae, a free holder to be his guardian. He is very sincere because of his worries of losing his family and them being sold away. I know the feeling of having lost my father Rueben being sold away. He was sold from his original family in North Carolina. The good Lord saw fit for him to meet my mama Tamar and find love only to be sold away again. I'm told he ended up in the west, no one knows. I may never see him on this side of the earth. Hopefully I see him in glory.

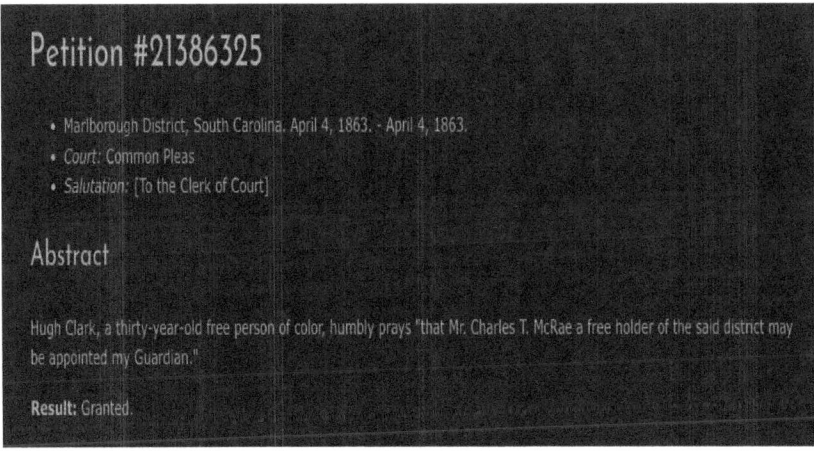

Petition #21386325

- Marlborough District, South Carolina. April 4, 1863. - April 4, 1863.
- Court: Common Pleas
- Salutation: [To the Clerk of Court]

Abstract

Hugh Clark, a thirty-year-old free person of color, humbly prays "that Mr. Charles T. McRae a free holder of the said district may be appointed my Guardian."

Result: Granted.

❖ Alex's son, Jacob, gives an account of what happens to Ruben in a book showcasing the lives of African American. Ruben may have joined the war efforts and fought for the union.

Name	Reuben Gordon
Side	Union
Regiment State/Origin	U.S. Colored Troops
Regiment	71st Regiment, United States Colored Infantry
Company	D
Rank In	Private
Rank Out	Private
Notes	See also 71 U.S.C.T.
Film Number	M589 roll 33
Memorial	Part of the African American Civil War Memorial
Plaque Number	C-79
Displayed As	Reuben Gordon

Jane Betty Kollock circa 1850

I watch my son, Jacob, have a faraway look in his eyes. I know he wants to leave here, this place is full of pain and old memories. I'm afraid that Alex is going to push him away. All of the other children are leaving here going to study at Biddle University, The young girls are going to Barbara Scotia Seminary. Alex, my sweet husband, can't shake his days at master Hubbard Plantation. I don't think he ever thought he would taste freedom. I believe he thinks they can take it away from him. Jacob knows freedom and can't remember being held in bondage. He has a quest to learn and can't understand why his father wants to hold him here. He wants to go away to study. I can't hold him back here if the good Lord wants him to go.

- ❖ Jane Betty's husband Alex was listed in a schedule of William Hubbard to be divided between his family after his death,
- ❖ The family's surname was changed from Kollock to Gordon
- ❖ Her son, Jacob, who later became Professor J.D Gordon attended college and became a teacher.

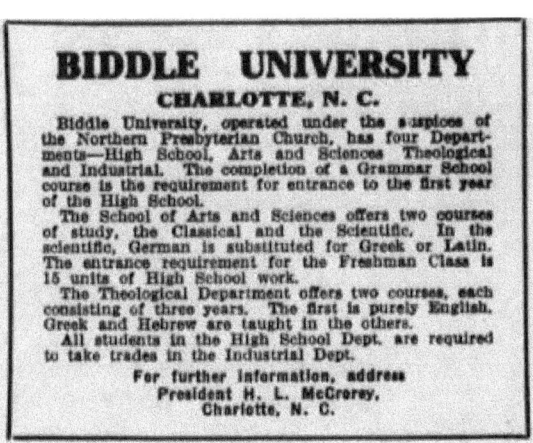

Walton-Raji

1850 Slave Schedule

In 1850, William Hubbard held twenty-eight slaves in Marlboro County.[1]

Gender Age Male 52 Male 48 Female 45 Female 35 Female 30 Female 25 Male 21 Male 21 Male 20 Male 18 Female 16 Female 17 Male 14 Male 12 Female 10 Female 10 Male 9 Male 9 Female 9 Male 7 Male 6 Male 5 Male 6 Male 4 Male 3 Male 2 Female 50 Female 4

Division of Slaves

William died intestate. An appraisement and division of land and slaves was completed December 24, 1857.[2] In November 1858, his widow, Honor, petitioned the court to be allowed to distribute the assets of the estate. The file was closed in December 1859.[3] The info below consolidates the info between the estate papers and an abstract of the petition.

Name	Est DOB	Enslavement Status	Color	Gender	Age in 1857	1858 Division	New Owner
Alexander ([Alick])	1841	slave	black	male	16	Lot 5	John Hubbard

(Gilbert *Slaves of William Hubbard, Marlboro County, South Carolina*)

Jane Bettie

BIRTH 1850 • South Carolina USA
DEATH , Marlboro, South Carolina, United States

3rd great-grandmother

Facts

Age 0 — **Birth**
1850 • South Carolina USA

Birth *(Alternate)*
abt 1847 • South Carolina USA

Age 12 — **Birth of daughter Julia Kollock Gordon** (1862–)
abt 1862 • , Marlboro, South Carolina, United States

Age 13 — **Birth of son Jacob D Gordon** (1863–)
Abt. 1863 • Cheraw, South Carolina

Age 20 — **Residence**
1870 • Smithville, Marlboro, South Carolina, USA
Residence Post Office: Bennettsville

Age 30 — **Residence**
1880 • Smithville, Marlboro, South Carolina, USA
Marital Status: Married; Relation to Head of House: Wife

Death
, Marlboro, South Carolina, United States

Family

Parents

Spouse and children

Alex Lalexis Gordon
1841–

Julia Kollock Gordon
1862–

Jacob D Gordon
1863–

Anna Harrington Gordon Part I

Jacob and I married in Concord, North Carolina. It's a big step in being able to get an education, being born right after slavery doesn't always make for a great life, but we were aiming to try. We were married by the Presbyterian minister. We had friends there to witness our nuptials. My neighbor Joe was there I have known him all my life. He's like a brother to me, and a friend to JD. People are looking at us to be a fine couple with us going to school and all. I went to Scotia Seminary and Jacob went to Biddle. We are pledged to serve our community, and I know the man that Jacob will help build schools in the area. Jacob, Professor Gordon, to others, and JD to me have done very well. He teaches at the local school, and is the superintendent of our church.

Name	Jacob D Gordon
Age in 1910	43
Birth Date	1867
Birthplace	South Carolina
Home in 1910	Concord Ward 4, Cabarrus, North Carolina, USA
Sheet Number	5a
Street	Broad St
House Number	67
Race	Colored (Black)
Gender	Male
Relation to Head of House	Head
Marital Status	Married
Spouse's Name	Annie L Gordon
Father's Birthplace	South Carolina
Mother's Birthplace	South Carolina
Native Tongue	English
Occupation	Teacher
Industry	Teaching School
Employer, Employee or Other	Wage Earner
Home Owned or Rented	Own
Home Free or Mortgaged	Free
Farm or House	House
Able to read	Y
Able to Write	Y
Enumeration District Number	0051
Years Married	20
Enumerated Year	1910

Professor Jacob Gordon courtesy of Denise M. McLain Library

Assistant Lore Local History Room Cabarrus County Public Library, Concord NC

Professor Jacob D. Gordon

A name is something that sets you apart from everyone else. How's your reputation, and your legacy? My father, Alex, changed ours from Kollock to Gordon like his fathers. My three sons have carried on that family name. All three had the opportunity to go to school and learn. I know that my leaving left Jimmy and Ludie at a disadvantage, but I planned to come back. I never meant to stay away. When I met Anna my life was so different from what I left behind in Cheraw. I wanted to be more than to be someone's human farming equipment on land I would never own. I guess it does not matter now. I'm losing the house, and I don't even want to face Anna. I carried her on my arm and made her high class, and now we are just getting by. Unfortunately, the name I'm so proud of my sons now are writing it on forms for a World War that we may not win.

   ❖ Jacob D. Gordon publicly acknowledged his family from his legal wife Anna L. Harrington, but not the children from his common-law wife Hattie Dumas.

Jacob Gordon sons

James "Jimmy"
William Ludie
John Verean

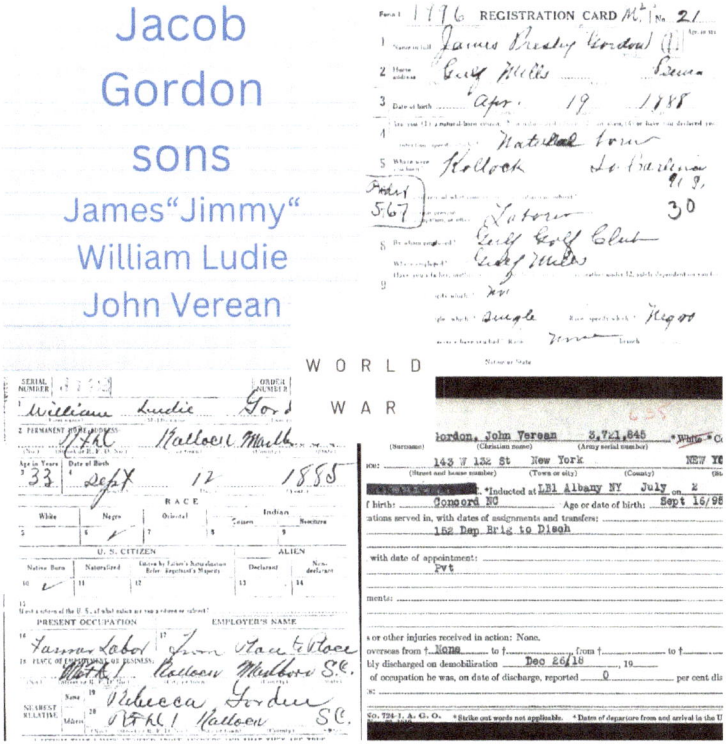

❖ Jacob publicly acknowledged his son with his wife Anna Harrington Gordon, but does not acknowledge his common law wife, Hattie Dumas of Marlboro, SC.

❖ He is rumored to have started families wherever he traveled.

Anna Harrington Jacob Gordon's second wife Part II

We've worked so hard living here. This place I call home is special to all of us here. In these walls, I've loved my family and educated my child. Jacob has been going all around town speaking and things are difficult with our home. In the world, he is a big important man who has accomplished so many things. We, like so many others, are broken. We can't keep up with the finances and owe so much. We may lose our home. Where will we go? How will others see us?

TRUSTEE'S SALE.

By virtue of authority vested in me by Deed in Trust or Mortgage executed by J. D. Gordon and wife, Annie L. Gordon on the 17th day of April, 1906, which Morgage or Deed in Trust is duly recorded in the Office of Register of Deeds for Cabarrus County, North Carolina, in Book No. 18, pages 260 to 261, and default having been made in payment thereof as therein provided; I will sell at public auction at the Court House Door in the City of Concord, North Carolina, on the 2nd day of August, 1915, at 12 o'clock m.,to the highest bidder for cash:

Elsie Harrington circa 1835

My girl Anna has married a good man. He's a good provider and takes care of her and Little Johnny. not many men would be willing to bring in their mother-in-law and their home and take care of them too. Many will turn them away and allow them to fend for themselves. I am glad he hasn't, I thank God for him. I know my daughter will be treated well.

Name	**Elsie Harrington**
Age in 1910	76
Birth Date	1834
Birthplace	South Carolina
Home in 1910	Concord Ward 4, Cabarrus, North Carolina, USA
Sheet Number	5a
Street	Broad St
Race	Colored (Black)
Gender	Female
Relation to Head of House	Mother-in-law
Marital Status	Widowed
Father's Birthplace	South Carolina
Mother's Birthplace	South Carolina
Native Tongue	English
Able to read	N
Able to Write	N
Enumeration District Number	0051
Number of Children Born	16
Number of Children Living	2
Enumerated Year	1910
Neighbors	View others on page

Household members

Name	Age
Jacob D Gordon	43
Annie L Gordon	39
John V Gordon	19
Elsie Harrington	76

Jacob D Gordon was profiled in a book of notable African Americans. The book is entitled <u>History of the American Negro and his institutions</u>; edited by A.B. Caldwell v. 4. It is from a book from the New York Public library, digitized by Google. His actual life account is added below.

Jacob Duckery Gordon

Prof. Jacob Duckery Gordon, one of the competent educators of North Carolina, comes to this State from South Carolina, having been born at Cheraw during the war, on August 9, 1864. His parents were Alexander and Jane (Ervin) Gordon. Alexander Gordon's father, Reuben, was brought from North to South Carolina and after years of service was again sold and carried west. His wife, Tamar, was the daughter of Jack and Maria Kollock. Prof. Gordon's mother was a daughter of Jacob Duckery and Juno Harrington. Thus it will be seen that he bears his grand-grandfather's name.

On December 23, 1888, our subject was married to Miss Anna Lillie Harrington, a daughter of John and Elsie Harrington. They have one son, John Vereen Gordon.

Those who are familiar with the history of the slave States know what a struggle the colored boys who were born in slavery or just after the war, had to secure an education. Prof. Gordon was no exception to the rule. His story cannot better be told than in his own simple language:

"I began school life in 1870. I learned my alphabet before the close of the first day in school and a happier soul never existed before nor since. My tutor was the son of an ex-salveholder and his children were in the school with us. I was very much in earnest about learning. At that time my highest ambition was to learn to read the Bible, so that I could join my great-grandfather, Jack, in reading about Joshua and the Amorites, Samson killing so many people with the jawbone of an ass and many other familiar stories. My father, although unlettered, was very much interested in the education of his children, but at the close of the short school term he did not care to see us use our books too much, especially when the grass was growing. This handicapped me and it was only when he was absent that I was able to study. Under these circumstances and without

History of the American Negro and his institutions;
edited by A.B. Caldwell
v. 4

the aid of a teacher, I learned to work vulgar fractions, denominate numbers and so on. I was very careful not to erase the copies which my teachers wrote for me on the last days of school, but would preserve them and write and re-write from them throughout the entire vacation. The day on which I learned to read, I ran ahead of all the other children to tell my mother and to read to her a few simple sentences. She was as proud of it as I was. My mother died in 1877 and father lost interest in me and my only sister, who was two years my senior. She married young and I went to live with her. I had now quit the old field school and was a student of Col. H. L. Shrewsburg, where I studied for two or three terms. My uncles, seeing my determination, induced me to save money to go to Biddle University. I hired to a farmer at seven dollars a month and in the fall of 1880 entered Biddle with $25.00 in cash. I remained until this was exhausted, borrowed railroad fare and returned. On reaching home I learned from my father that he had not sent me any money for the reason that the man for whom he was working had refused to pay him any money when he learned that it was to go for the education of his son. Instead of being discouraged, this spurred me to greater efforts and I was now more determined than ever to obtain an education. The following year I returned to college and at the end of the term thought I was 'some scholar' and was eager to begin teaching. I was discouraged on the ground that I was too young and did not begin teaching until two years later. In 1884 I began in Marborough Co. and remained there for eleven consecutive years."

In 1885, Prof. Gordon went to Palatka, Florida, and began merchandising, but did not find that kind of work congenial so at the end of the year he returned to South Carolina and resumed teaching. In 1894 he was on the Grand Jury of the U. S. District Court. Following that he moved to Concord, N. C., where he has since remained. His principal work since he came to the Old North State has been teaching though he has been active in other fields

History of the American Negro and his institutions;

edited by A.B. Caldwell v. 4

as well. He is now (1920) serving his eleventh year as assistant principal of the Concord Colored Graded & Industrial School.

When the Coleman Manufacturing Company erected at Concord a cotton mill to be operated entirely by colored people, Prof. Gordon found employment there during his vacations as a private secretary. In 1919 the Colored Division of the Textile Workers of America was organized at Concord and Prof. Gordon was elected Financial Secretary, which position he has held since. In October of the same year he was elected delegate to the annual meeting of the Textile Workers which was held in Baltimore, and was the only person of color present and the only colored union representative out of the 200 delegates from fifteen States. His position as an educator in the county may be seen from the fact that he is President of the Colored County Teachers' Association. Prof. Gordon is a member of the A. M. E. Zion church and is President of the Sunday School Union of Concord, and was for two years District Sunday School Superintendent of the Concord District.

He has found particular help and inspiration in reading the lives of Lincoln, Grant, Garfield, Fred Douglas and others. With the years has come success not only in his chosen profession but in a business and financial way as well. He has accumulated considerable property in and around Concord so that his annual taxes amount to at least $100.00.

Julia Milton circa 1900

I just don't understand people. We are still grieving because my daughter Lethia Mae. Her cousin Hannah has gone and married her husband. I knew the girls were close. The two of them grew up the best of friends laughing and talking all the time. Leitha had a stroke, and needed a lot of help. Hannah was over there giving a helping hand. My baby girl just left us in February, here it is November and Hannah has married my daughter's husband. I was worried about my girl marrying a soldier. Who knows what family he left behind somewhere, or going back to. It makes me wonder if they were seeing each other while my daughter was on her sick bed.

Photo is from an online collection from the grandchild of Matthew Bass.

Certificate of Marriage, Commonwealth of Virginia — No. 2616. City or County: Newport News. Full Name of Groom: Matthew Bass. Present Name of Bride: Lethia Mae Kollock. Maiden Name: Lethia Mae Kollock. Groom: Age 32, col., single, none. Bride: Age 22, col., single, none. Occupation: Soldier, U.S. Army. Bride Occupation: Waitress, Peoples Cafe. Birthplace: St. Joseph, La. Bride Birthplace: Bennettsville, S. C. Father's Full Name: John Bass. Bride's Father's Full Name: Sudberry Kollock. Mother's Maiden Name: Surtila Kenedy. Bride's Mother's Maiden Name: Julia Mitton. Residence: Camp Patrick Henry, Va. Bride Residence: 612 - 17 St., Newport News, Va. Date of Proposed Marriage: February 7, 1944. Place of Proposed Marriage: Newport News, Va. Given under my hand this 7th day of February, 19 44. F. B. Barham, Deputy Clerk of Corporation Court.

Certificate of Date and Place of Marriage. I, R.A.T. Clement acting by authority of Court Appointment, do certify that on the 7th day of Feb'y, 1944, at Newport News, Virginia, under authority of this license, I joined together in the Holy State of Matrimony the persons named and described therein. I qualified and gave bond according to law authorizing me to celebrate the rites of marriage in the county (or city) of Newport News, Commonwealth of Virginia. Given under my hand this 7th day of February, 19 44. Address of celebrant #236-25th St., Newport News, Va. Court Appointee.

Hannah Barnes

I know my cousins Shrusberry and Julia don't understand my choice for marrying Matthew. After losing Lethia we were so lost in our grief, we needed someone to understand. I did everything I could to help my cousin while she was alive. She asked me to look after Matthew when she was gone. I never knew that I would end up looking after his heart too. Yes he is older, but he is a good man, and I know he will be good to me. My family loves him for how good he was to his first wife. They know when I am with him I will be loved and in great care. Maybe in time they will see I wouldn't have done anything to hurt my cousin, or the same family. Love is love that is all I know.

Leitha Mae Kollock

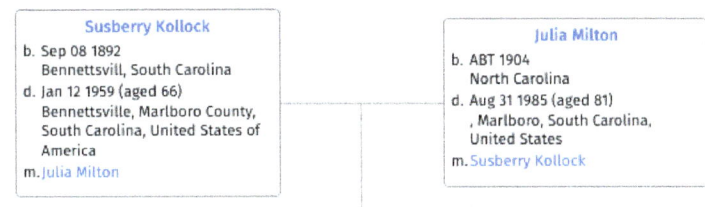

Susberry Kollock
b. Sep 08 1892
  Bennettsvill, South Carolina
d. Jan 12 1959 (aged 66)
  Bennettsville, Marlboro County,
  South Carolina, United States of
  America
m. Julia Milton

Julia Milton
b. ABT 1904
  North Carolina
d. Aug 31 1985 (aged 81)
  , Marlboro, South Carolina,
  United States
m. Susberry Kollock

Lethia Mae Kollock
b. 1923
  Bennettsville, Marlboro County, South
  Carolina, United States of America
d. Feb 18 1949 (aged 26)
  Bennettsville, Marlboro County, South
  Carolina, United States of America
e. Burial
  Wallace, Marlboro County, South Carolina,
  United States of America
m. Matthew Bass
  Newport News, Virginia, USA
  d. Feb 12 1991
m. Booker T Harrington
  d. Jan 1988

Hannah Barnes

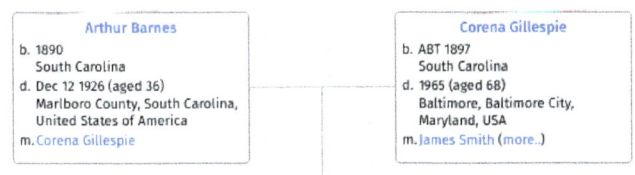

Arthur Barnes
b. 1890
  South Carolina
d. Dec 12 1926 (aged 36)
  Marlboro County, South Carolina,
  United States of America
m. Corena Gillespie

Corena Gillespie
b. ABT 1897
  South Carolina
d. 1965 (aged 68)
  Baltimore, Baltimore City,
  Maryland, USA
m. James Smith (more...)

Hannah Barnes
b. ABT 1928
  South Carolina
d. Apr 07 2009 (aged 81)
  Michigan, USA
e. Residence
  1930
  Kollock, Marlboro, South Carolina, USA
  Marital Status: Single; Relation to Head:
  Daughter
m. Matthew Bass
  d. Feb 12 1991

Priscilia Gillespie Part I

My cousin James and his wife Lottie son John Birks is really doing things up north. He is playing that horn all over the United States and out of the country. They named some apartments after him over in Cheraw. That is right nice. I know James was a hard man, but seeing his boy do so well with the music he taught him would have softened him up. He would have been so proud of his youngest son. It is a shame he never got to see what he had become.

John Birks Gillespie's Parents

James Penifeild Gillespie with wife Lottie Powe Gillespie

G.   JACE. "A Bass Photo Album." *Classical Music Forum*,

Talk Classical, 27 Sept. 2016,

125

MRS. LOTTIE GILLESPIE MOTHER OF MUSICIAN "DIZZY GILLESPIE, DEAD

Mrs. Lottie (Poe) Gillespie, mother of famed "bebop" musician John "Dizzy" Gillespie of New York City, died in the Springfield Hospital late Wednesday after a brief illness.

She was born in Cheraw, S. C., and had lived in Springfield for the past six years.

Her trumpet-playing son, a top name in the jazz field, made his mark as a leading exponent of the "bebop" school.

"Lottie Gillespie" Newspapers.com, Transcript-Telegram, November 21, 1959, https://www.newspapers.com/article/transcript-telegram-lottie-gillespie/146180882/

Mrs. Alice Wilson

Cheraw, SC

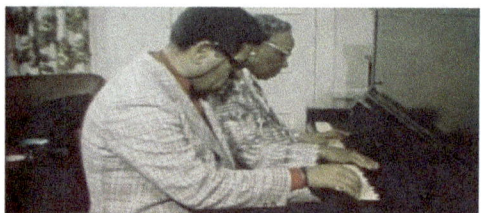

All Photos features on this page are from a documentary written, produced and narrated by Zane Knauss

Mrs. McDuffie

Lauringburg NC

Dizzy remembered in native Cheraw

DIZZY GILLESPIE

CHERAW (AP) — Famed jazz trumpeter Dizzy Gillespie got his start as a showman in the third grade, when he fell in love with a friend's new trumpet.

But he responded to all kinds of musical activities when he was in grade school, a former teacher, Alice Wilson, told the Florence Morning News.

Gillespie, 75, died Wednesday in an Englewood, N.J., hospital where he was being treated for pancreatic cancer.

Born John Birks Gillespie in Cheraw, he helped popularize jazz through a combination of humor and showmanship and his trademark bulging cheeks and bent trumpet.

His start came in third grade, when he played a friend's new trumpet whenever he could.

"We used to practice on that trumpet so much, double-timing it, it's a wonder we didn't wear out the horn," he wrote in his memoirs, "To Be or Not to Bop."

Wilson, 92, remembered Gillespie's love of music from when she taught him in the third and fourth grades at the former Robert Smalls Grade School in Cheraw.

Gillespie enjoyed helping out whenever the teacher led extra-curricular activities that involved music, she said.

"We had a group that was learning how to play music and he would always be in the shows," she said. "Anything I wanted to do musically, he would do it. He would pay more attention to his horn than his books."

Wilson said Gillespie always visited her when he returned to Cheraw, which sports a sign reading, "Home of Dizzy Gillespie."

The local arts council uses his trademark horn, with its bell

(See Remembered, page 2)

TRUMPET MASTER DEAD AT 75

ENGLEWOOD, N.J. (AP) — The death of Dizzy Gillespie silenced an original — a musical one-of-a-kind in everything from his cool bebop rhythms to his stage antics, his bullfrog cheeks and his bent trumpet.

The legendary horn player died at age 75 Wednesday at Englewood Hospital and Medical Center, where he was being treated for pancreatic cancer. His music was playing when he died, said Virginia Wicks, his spokeswoman.

"He must know that he has given more pleasure to more people than most people get to do in a lifetime," said jazz vocalist Joe Williams. "Watching him was like watching a magician."

Gillespie stood in the forefront of jazz for decades, giving shape in the 1940s to the raucous jazz re-invention he named bebop and later merging Latin rhythms with mainstream jazz. Bandleader Woody Herman ranked Gillespie with Louis Armstrong as the most influential jazz musicians of all time.

"He is a father of modern jazz," said jazz vibraphonist Lionel Hampton. "There are lots of music styles in jazz but only one

(See Dizzy, page 2)

"Dizzy Gillespie Remembered " Newspapers.com, The Index-Journal, January 7, 1993, https://www.newspapers.com/article/the-index-journal-dizzy-gillespie-rember/132148176/

WOMAN WHO SAYS SHE'S DIZZY GILLESPIE'S CHILD SUES

NEW YORK — A woman who claims to be the illegitimate daughter of Dizzy Gillespie has filed a lawsuit against the jazz great's widow and a music compa-

Dizzy Gillespie greeting fellow musician Benny Carter, 1948. Allan Grant / The LIFE Picture Collection Photos of Dizzy in black and white

Remembering Dizzy in the centennial year of his birth By HOWARD REICH PUBLISHED: May 8, 2017 UPDATED: May 8, 2019

Priscilia Gillespie part II

People around here see me in one or two ways.They either love me or hate me. I'm always the topic of conversation, but this time it is not me. They are talking about my sister Hattie. First, she had a child with Jimmy, my daughter's father, now she has gone so far as to marry him. I know that we weren't together anymore, but she still should have known that stuff like this breaks up families. I guess we will have to raise our children as cousins instead of brothers or sisters. It is her cross to bear, not mine. The other sisters are angry and are wondering if she will be looking at their men too. I know it isn't easy being a woman all on her own. I hadn't gotten over her getting a baby from him. How can I get over her marrying him?

Priscilla Gillespie

Gillespie family recorded in a Bible from the Henry Harrington Plantation

The Gillespie Sisters
Marlboro County SC, children of former slaves

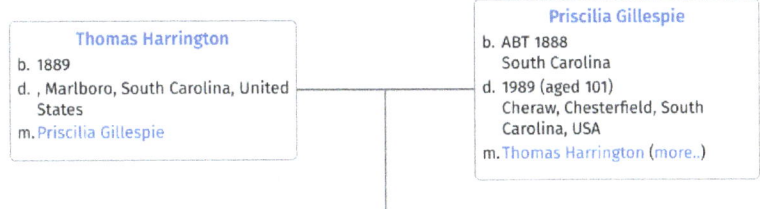

Thomas Harrington

b. 1889
d. , Marlboro, South Carolina, United
States
m. Priscilia Gillespie

Priscilia Gillespie

b. ABT 1888
South Carolina
d. 1989 (aged 101)
Cheraw, Chesterfield, South
Carolina, USA
m. Thomas Harrington (more..)

Sillar Gertude Harrington

b. ABT 1922
Bennettsville, Marlboro, South Carolina,
USA
d. Dec 03 2005 (aged 83)
Bennettsville, Marlboro, South Carolina
e. Residence
1935
Whites Creek, Marlboro, South Carolina
m. Brimal M. Easterling
d. May 13 2005

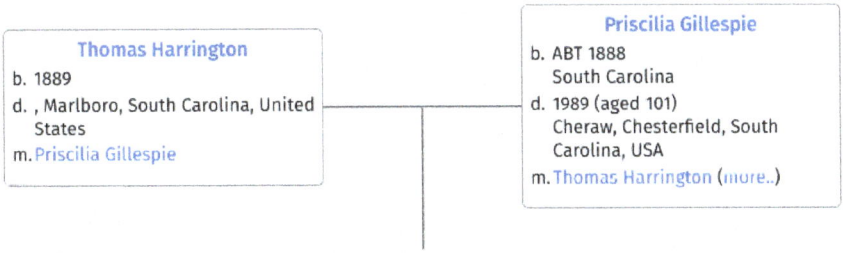

Thomas Harrington

b. 1889
d. , Marlboro, South Carolina, United
States
m. Priscilia Gillespie

Priscilia Gillespie

b. ABT 1888
South Carolina
d. 1989 (aged 101)
Cheraw, Chesterfield, South
Carolina, USA
m. Thomas Harrington (more..)

Hattie Harrington

b. Nov 07 1912
Bennettsville, Marlboro, South Carolina,
USA
d. , Marlboro, South Carolina, United States
m. Jasper Strong

Sillar Gertude Harrington

Lord, I have been praying for my sister Hattie. The sheriff has been back and forth over to her house before and after what happened to Jasper. Her husband, Jasper Short, has been missing for days. People started talking about the smell around the house. Well they found him, he was under the porch, and my sister doesn't look like a grieving widow. That sheriff does not look too concerned especially when he came out the house smoking one of Jasper's pipes.

❖ Sillar Gertude's brother-in-law was found under the porch with a stab wound in his chest. Family lore states that his wife, Hattie Harrington Strong, was having an affair with the sheriff and nothing was done concerning his death.

❖ Hattie Harrington and Sillar Gertude Harrington were daughters of Priscilla.

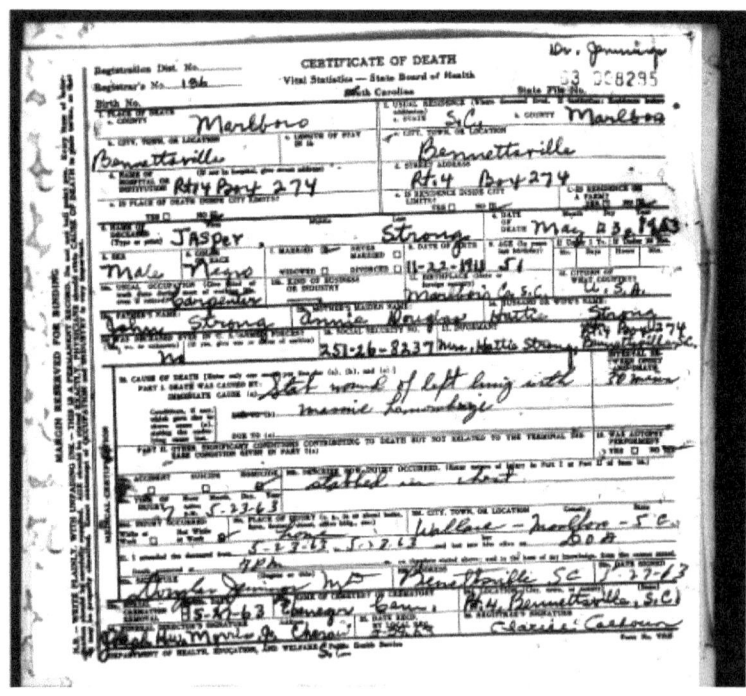

Timothy Quick

I have just started towards the house with my horse and wagon. The weather is mighty cold, but I don't have far to go. I just left my cousin Pearline's house and had some Press Gordon spirits to taste. The liquor has warmed me right up and will allow me to turn out Hattie Short's house. Her family is one of those Gillespie women and people say they are right crazy. I must be a little crazy too, I'm staying in her house and the rumor is that she killed her husband. The folks here told me if she took her husband then she would take me too. They said the sheriff did not do anything about it. Some say they were sweet on each other. I don't mind any of what people are saying, as long she is always alright with me. I pay to stay here by the month and I don't get in the way of her love life.

Hattie Rebecca Gillespie

My nephew Roman brought my sister Lottie up here from Clio to sit awhile. The more I see that boy the more he looks like a Gordon. There is no denying that William Ludie is his daddy. We talked about old times, and laughed a while. I miss my sister, something terrible, everybody else is just a piece of the way down the road, but I miss talking to her.

Photos are from a collection by her descendant Lillie Chrisitan

Daughter of Andrew Gillespie and Elizabeth Harrington Gillespie. She was sister to Pricillia Gillespie, and wife to James Presley Gordon Sr.

Lottie Gillespie with son Roman

I was riding home to Clio from visiting my sister Hattie over in the sandhills of Kollock, SC with Roman. We got right in the heart of Bennettsville when I looked over at that big old colored church called Shiloh Baptist Church. The clouds had darkened like a storm was coming and it had started to rain a little bit. A couple of little children were playing in their Sunday clothes. They were just laughing and running around getting dirty. I can imagine that they already smell like outside. The little children don't realize there are two things you don't mess with: God while he's working, and a southern black woman on a Sunday.

❖ One of Shiloh's past pastors Arthur Jermone Wright and his first lady was a piano teacher. The couple opened the first home for the elderly in Bennettsville SC to anyone who needed care.

❖ Their daughter, Marian Wright was the first black woman to pass the Mississippi bar. She worked as an aid for Dr. Martin Luther King Jr, and founded The Washing Research Project, and The Children's Defense Fund to aid children. In later years the library in her hometown was named after her.

Rev. Wright and wife Maggie sit outside of one of their residences for the elderly in the community. This photo was obtained from the Marlboro County Museum Facebook page on Feb 15, 22

City Native, Former King Aide Are Wed

McLEAN, Va. (AP) — Peter Edelman, 30, a native of Minneapolis and a former adviser to the late Sen. Robert F. Kennedy, and Marion Wright, 29, a close friend of Dr. Martin Luther King Jr., the slain civil rights leader, were married Sunday in a simple ceremony here.

(Edelman is the son of Mr. and Mrs. Hyman Edelman, 4816 W. Lake Harriet Blvd. His father is a member of the law firm of Maslon, Kaplon, Edelman and Borman.)

The marriage was performed by the Rev. William Sloane Coffin, 44, chaplain of Yale University who was found guilty last month with Dr. Benjamin Spock and others of conspiring to counsel evasion of the draft.

Court, told the couple — whose lives had been touched by the assassinations of King and Kennedy — it was not "easy" in such a year to celebrate an event of joy.

The bride, born in Bennettsville, S.C., was graduated from Yale School and was the first Negro admitted to the bar in Mississippi. She handled cases for the NAACP legal defense fund and worked for the Southern Christian Leadership Conference during the Poor People's Campaign.

Edelman is a former official in the Justice Department.

MARIAN WRIGHT ELDERMAN

PIONEER

30 p.m.: Marian Wright Elderman of National Children's Defense Fund will in Love Auditorium on the campus of son College, followed by a reception ook signing. For more information, (__) 999-2225

Marian Wright Edelman national portrait Artist Ruven Afanador,
born 22 Oct 1959

James Presley Gordon

Johnny is around here aggravating those girls. I got a house full of girls and one boy that lives here. It always seems like he wants to get next to their nerves. I know that I don't always do things right, but I'm trying. On my good days, I hope they see it. On my bad days, I hope they forgive me. There is no guide on how to do this family thing right. My family didn't have a good start. My grandfather Professor Gordon left my father behind., which made him a hard man. I tried to keep things together. My first marriage, well we both messed that up. I have to do this marriage differently. I want my son to see the best.

- ❖ John Gordon plays with his sisters. Photo is from a collection of photos shared.
- ❖ Oral family history notes that he was a hard working man that believed in working for himself, and living off his own land.

James Presley Gordon Sr. (Father)marriage to Hattie Gillespie

MARRIAGE LICENSE
AFFIDAVIT TO OBTAIN LICENSE

STATE OF SOUTH CAROLINA,
County of Marlboro

I do hereby solemnly swear that I am legally capacitated to marry; that my full name is
James P Gordon
that my age is 31 years and months; my place of residence is
Kollock SC my race is Negro
my nationality is American
SWORN to before me this 19 day of Jun A.D. 19 17
(L. S.) J M Hawley
Notary Public. James P Gordon

MARRIAGE LICENSE

STATE OF SOUTH CAROLINA
County of Marlboro

I do solemnly swear that I am legally capicitated to marry; that my full name is
Hattie Gillespie
that my age is 21 years and months; my place of residence is
Kollock SC ; my race is Negro
my nationality is American
SWORN to before me this 19 day of Jun A.D. 19 19
(L. S.) J M Hawley
Notary Public. Hattie Gillespie

MARRIAGE LICENSE

STATE OF SOUTH CAROLINA,
County of Marlboro

WHEREAS, It has been made to appear to me, J. G. McLaurin, Judge of Probate for Marlboro County, upon oath
that Jas P Gordon of Kollock SC
and Hattie Gillespie of
are legally capacitated to contract matrimony, and that their ages are respectively 31 years and
months, and 21 years and months; and that their race is Negro
and their nationality is American

THESE are, therefore to authorize any person qualified to perform marriage ceremonies to perform the marriage ceremony for the persons above named, and for so doing this shall be sufficient warrant.

GIVEN under my Hand and Seal this 19 day of JUN 1918 A.D. 19
J G McLaurin, Probate Judge
Judge of Probate for Marlboro County.

Marriage record James P. Gordon Jr. (Son) to Hattie Tillman

MARRIAGE LICENSE
AFFIDAVITS TO OBTAIN LICENSE

STATE OF SOUTH CAROLINA.
COUNTY OF MARLBORO

I do solemnly swear that I am legally capacitated to marry; that my full name is _James Presley Gordon, Jr._ ; that my age is _22_ years and _____ months; my place of residence is _Bennettsville, S.C. R # 4_ ; my race is _Colored_ ; my nationality is American.

SWORN to before me this _23rd._ day of _January_ A. D. 194_3_

J. F. Kinney (L. S.)
Notary Public for S. C.

James P Gordon Jr

STATE OF SOUTH CAROLINA.
COUNTY OF MARLBORO

I do solemnly swear that I am legally capacitated to marry; that my full name is _Hattie Mae Tillman_ ; that my age is _21_ years and _____ months; my place of residence is _Hamlet, N.C. Route # 2_ ; my race is _Colored_ ; my nationality is American.

SWORN to before me this _23 d._ day of _January_ A. D. 1943

J. F. Kinney (L. S.)
Notary Public for S. C.

Hattie Mae Tillman

Marriage License

STATE OF SOUTH CAROLINA.
COUNTY OF MARLBORO.

WHEREAS, IT HAS BEEN MADE TO APPEAR TO ME, JOHN F. KINNEY, JUDGE OF PROBATE FOR MARLBORO COUNTY, UPON OATH, THAT:

James Presley Gordon, Jr. of _Bennettsville,S.C.- R # 4_
and _Hattie Mae Tillman_ of _Hamlet,N.C. - R # 2_

are legally capacitated to contract matrimony, and that their ages are respectively _22_ years and _____ months and _21_ years and _____ months, and their race is _Colored_ and their nationality is American.

These are, therefore, to authorize any person qualified to perform marriage ceremonies to perform the marriage ceremony for the persons above named and for so doing this shall be sufficient warrant.

Given under my Hand and Seal this _23rd_ day of _January_ A. D. 194_3_

John F. Kinney
Judge of Probate for Marlboro County.

Marriage of James P. Gordon (Son) to Carrie Fair

MARRIAGE LICENSE

AFFIDAVITS TO OBTAIN LICENSE

No. 52593

STATE OF SOUTH CAROLINA,
COUNTY OF MARLBORO (*Gordon*)

I do solemnly swear that I am legally capacitated to marry; that my full name is _James Presley Gordon, Jr._ ; that my age is _26_ years and _____ months; my place of residence is _Bennettsville, S.C._ ; my race is _Negro_ ; my nationality is American.

SWORN to before me this _3rd_ day of _May_ A. D. 194_7_ (L. S.)

J. F. Kinney
Notary Public for S. C.

James P Gordon Jr

STATE OF SOUTH CAROLINA,
COUNTY OF MARLBORO

I do solemnly swear that I am legally capacitated to marry; that my full name is _Carrie Pearline Fair_ ; that my age is _23_ years and _____ months; my place of residence is _Hamlet, N.C._ ; my race is _Negro_ ; my nationality is American.

SWORN to before me this _3rd_ day of _May_ A. D. 194_7_ (L. S.)

J. F. Kinney
Notary Public for S. C.

Carrie P Fair

STATE OF SOUTH CAROLINA,
COUNTY OF MARLBORO.

Marriage License

WHEREAS, IT HAS BEEN MADE TO APPEAR TO ME, JOHN F. KINNEY, JUDGE OF PROBATE FOR MARLBORO COUNTY, UPON OATH AND PURSUANT TO AN APPLICATION IN WRITING FILED ON ___2nd_ DAY OF _May_ 194_7_ AT _10:55_ A.M. THAT:

James Presley Gordon, Jr. of _Bennettsville, S.C._

and _Carrie Pearline Fair_ of _Hamlet, N.C._

are legally capacitated to contract matrimony, and their ages are respectively _26_ years and _____ months and _23_ years and _____ months, and their race is _Negro_ and their nationality is American.

These are, therefore, to authorize any person qualified to perform marriage ceremonies to perform the marriage ceremony for the persons above named and for so doing this shall be sufficient warrant.

Given under my Hand and Seal this _3rd_ day of _May_ A. D. 194_7_

at _8:00_ P.M.
8:00

John F. Kinney
Judge of Probate for Marlboro County

Carrie Pearline Fair Part I

The fourth of July is here and my children and I always celebrate with a big cookout at the state park. The grandchildren often go out to the waterfall, while their parents and I sit and talk. I'm afraid they will step on something, or get too close to the water. The bigger boy plays basketball on the court. The smaller children are playing hopscotch on the sidewalks until they can go get in the water. The park is full today, families are everywhere. It is good to see so many people out here laughing, and enjoying each other without any arguing and fussing.

Newspaper clipping from, The Cheraw Chronicle, of the family having a cookout at Cheraw State Park. The date of the article is unknown. The basketball, and hop stock areas are no longer there. Improvements were made in other areas of the park.

Carrie Pearline Fair Part II

I have called those grandchildren in from outside three times to get them to eat something. At least they have stopped long enough to get some water for a few times. The playhouse is all the grands talk about. For somebody passing by it is a spot in the woods, to my grandchildren it is home to their imagination. The yells and screams of laughter are all that I hear. I know they are alright! The sandhills are good to them. I guess I will turn off this floor model tv and go sit on this porch and listen to them. A couple of them are playing church in the front, singing and shouting and carrying on. The boys are playing cowboys. Two of the girls got pine cones and magnolia leaves talking about chicken and collard greens. If I can get them to eat some real food I'll be satisfied. I guess I'll let them play as long as they can.

CARRIE P FAIR

Loving

Provider
Loyal
Family first

John "Johnny" Gordon

Today Mr. Amos Boatwright came to the house already drunk. Daddy had gone to town. Mama was in the house cooking supper. The girls were outside talking under a tree. I saw him first, staggering as he walked yelling for Daddy. I knew Mama wouldn't want to deal with him so I tried to stop him before he got all the way in the yard. I threw the sticks I had in my hand to get his attention. He called me a little pickaninny and told me was going to bust me up the side of my head if I threw another stick at him. I believed he would try, but was too drunk to catch me. I laughed and stuck out my tongue at him. He swung his large dark hand to swat at me. He missed and swung all the way around. In his drunken state, he fell to the ground. He yelled out cussing at me, God, and Mama. His actions alerted the girls who came running. My oldest sister spoke first asking him if he was alright. I told her he was fine, that he was trying to hurt me. Mr. Amos started mumbling something about stump. Mama came out of the house and walked fast. He looked at Mama and said," Hey Pearl, stump stump stump." Mama frowned her face and said, "You drunk enough, ain't no stump liquor here. Go on home now.' The man started to cry saying, "Pearl I'm sorry, I ain't

148

never hurt nobody. I love everybody. I love the Lord. " Mama told him it was good that he loved God, and that God loved him. The man shook his head in agreement trying to stand to his feet. When he realized that he couldn't stand he cursed Mama for hiding liquor and our absent daddy for telling her to do it. Mama told him again to go home.

He told her he would leave when Daddy came home. With great effort, Mr. Boatwright made his way to his feet and walked to the porch. We all watched as he sat in a chair and quickly drifted off to sleep. When Daddy got home that night he saw Mr. Boatwright was still asleep on the porch and called him an old fool and went on into the house.

❖ This story was completely fictional, but based on oral traditional stories of my father John Gordon. He spoke of men coming to my grandparent's home to buy the corn whiskey my grandfather made. From my research on census records, there wasn't anyone named Amos Boatwright in the North and South Carolina border. I chose the name Boatwright because there were several family lines that carry that surname.

Caston Lacosta Gordon

Caston Gordon sits mid center holding the cigarette

Leaving Marlboro South Carolina has been great for me. There I am not reduced to glares and assumptions. I am free to live my life in the way that is comfortable to me. Yes I am from southern dirt roads, most days were horrible. My father Jimmy was too strict and stuck in his ways. My older brother James is starting to act like him and be critical of my choices. In New York I can reinvent myself, and live a classy life. Wine and dine, and live life to fullest. Farming and sharecropping. I'm done with all of that.

Carrie Pearline Fair Part III

Press' father Mr. Jimmy Gordon has passed on. It is rather hard for them being that they lost their mother Miss Hattie a while back. Theodore is his youngest and seems a little lost with his father gone. He is going to stay with us for a while. My children are still quite young and he may be able to help Press out around here with some things when he gets out of school.

Rufus T. Gordon

❖ Census records have Theodore living in the home of his older brother and sister-in-law when he was still a teenager.

Carrie Pearline Fair Part IV

The schools have integrated. The older girls went to EastSide High in Bennettsville, SC. The younger children are going to Kollock School and their Mascot is a Bearcat. Johnny is playing football and playing in the band. He talks about his history teacher Mr. Crosland, his band teacher Mr. Spears and his cousin Mrs. Hudson. It is always good to have family members keeping their eyes on your children. I know she won't let them get out of hand in any way.

Dedicated educator Annie Gillespie Hudson taught for thirty nine years.

Birthday observed: Mrs. Annie G. Hudson was given a surprise birthday dinner in the educational building at the Cheraw United Presbyterian Church. The dinner was planned by her daughter, Mrs. Cecelia Davis, and sister, Miss G. E. Gillespie, and other friends. The dinner was served to all church members and friends who wished to remain after

Rosanna Boatwright

Today is another day that my breathing is hard. I am trying my best to maintain it, but my days are hard. I am trying all of the remedies I can like homemade teas, wines, and broths, but most days I can't make it through before the pain and the coughing spells return. Johnny is afraid that if I ever close my eyes I won't ever open them. I keep telling him, nothing is going to happen to me.

❖ Rosanna Kollock Boatwright passed away from lung cancer. There aren't any oral histories that note her trying to restore her health. Most southern people try different remedies to heal themselves.

Jane James Harrington

It has been a dry season. The sky did not yield as much rain as the season needed. The vegetables aren't as plentiful and there are many mouths to feed. The children are working on the off season and a few are in school. Our oldest girl has come back home bringing her baby with her. I know that she's prideful and doesn't want to admit her need, and feel that she has failed. We have all been there a time or two. We have all been down on our luck. Families support each other, that's what families are supposed to do. We will always be there for each other.

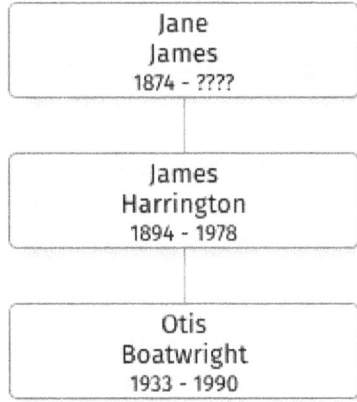

Relationship Summary

Jane James's grandson is **Otis Boatwright**

Otis Boatwright

We have moved from Old Wire Road to Brickyard Road in Wallace. Mama isn't feeling her best these days. She's not able to work, so I do all of the farm work that I can. She has so much on her mind she seems to get confused. When she was up and going she was something else. I wish I could see her well. Grandma Rosana is having to keep everyone up and going. We don't have much but we get by with what we have.

Name	Velma Boatwright
Age	37
Birth Date	abt 1913
Gender	Female
Race	Negro (Black)
Birth Place	South Carolina
Marital Status	Never Married (Single)
Relation to Head of House	Daughter
Residence Date	1950
Home in 1950	Kollock, Marlboro, South Carolina, USA
Street Name	Old Wire Road
Apartment Number	On Left
Dwelling Number	149
Farm	No
Acres	No
Occupation Category	Unable to Work

Otis went on to have an impressive military career.

Neighbors of Jane James

Augusta, Carolina, and Brown Gillespie walk side by side leaving their white folk's homes. Augusta was born in Carolina and has never known Georgia soil. truly none of us have ever seen any other soil. We were brought here to farm, breed and die. Whether we were slave, free, young, or old our days are mostly the same. We tell our days and nights from the sun and the moon. We feel the change of the seasons from the heat on our back in the summer fields and the cold in our bones in the winter. We are as much part of God's nature as the grass and trees. Our blood, sweat, and tears have dropped, poured, and spilled on these grounds.

Mary Harrington circa 1825

Dinah Harrington, Mike's mama, is worrisome today. The children had a little cough and she is bringing in those home remedies of the old Africans on the plantation. Those people are from a different time, and a different way. We are all mixed up down here, whatever they used over there may not work over here. I'd rather go talk to people here and see what they may be using. This new way may be better than the old. If that doesn't work, I guess I'll use what she has at least for her to hush a little while. Yesterday she complained that I did not have enough lye in the clothes when I washed them. The day before that I did not have enough sugar in the hoe cakes. The weather was not agreeable, and neither was she.

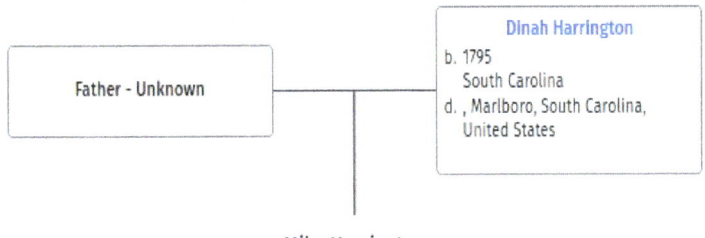

Mike Harrington

b. S. C.

e. Residence
   1870
   Smithville, Marlboro, South Carolina, USA
   Residence Post Office: Bennettsville

m. Mary Harrington

Diana Harrington

United States, Freedmen's Bureau Ration Records,1865-1872

Name:	Diana Harrington
Event Type:	Residence
Event Date:	1865-1872
Event Place:	Cheraw, Chesterfield, South Carolina, United States
Event Place (Original):	Marlboro
Gender:	Female
Age:	75
Race:	Colored
Race (Original):	Colored

Marlboro County African Born

We are the last of the old timers, the last of our kind. We are the last that know the old ways in these parts. The White Masters call us African darkies, but I call us survivors. We are built differently from the negros here. We know ways they've never seen. We have walked on lands that they laughed about. Their souls don't even remember. The last three recently died Duence, Flora, And Boston. We all left behind so many loved ones. They are from different plantations but in the same area. Now they're gone, and it's just me left. I am all that is left to carry the words, and traditions.

❖ All of the names list are from *Mortality Schedules, 1850-1885*

Children Playing

The children are playing in the Red Sand Hills of Wallace. Their laughter could be heard down the road. Neighbors and friends sit on their porches and listen in the distance. Each child represented a different family line. These children playing together surnames were Boatwright, Harrington, Kollock, and Quick. Each child descends from a different tribe ending up on American soil and the depths of Carolina.

❖ The names represented are surnames of enslavers of the Pee Dee area. Those enslaved were often sold, given as gifts, or willed to family members.

Name	**Geo R Boatwright**
Free or Enslaved	**Owner**
Event Type	**Census**
Event Date	**1860**
Event Place	**Chesterfield, South Carolina, United States**
Event Place (Original)	**Chesterfield, South Carolina**

Name	**J W Harrington**
Relationship to Owner	**Owner**
Event Type	**Census**
Event Date	**1850**
Event Place	**Marlboro, Marlboro, South Carolina, United States**
Event Place (Original)	**Marlboro county, Marlboro, South Carolina, United States**
Schedule Type	**1850 Slave Schedule**

Name	**O H Kollock**
Free or Enslaved	**Owner**
Event Type	**Census**
Event Date	**1860**
Event Place	**Marlboro, Marlboro, South Carolina, United States**
Event Place (Original)	**Marlbro, South Carolina**

Name	**Benjamin Quick**
Relationship to Owner	**Owner**
Event Type	**Census**
Event Date	**1850**
Event Place	**Marlboro, Marlboro, South Carolina, United States**
Event Place (Original)	**Marlboro county, Marlboro, South Carolina, United States**
Schedule Type	**1850 Slave Schedule**

Chesterfield County Highway Map

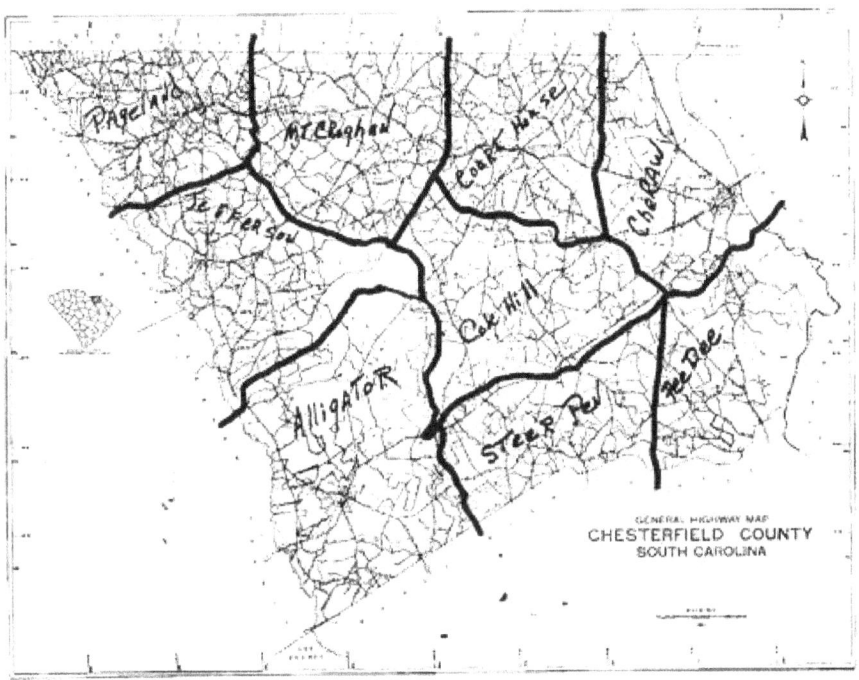

Townships in Chesterfield have remained basically the same except for Old Store, which is now Pageland

Map is from a collection by the Maples family.

Vaccinating Against Smallpox.

When Dr. A. H. Hayden, epidemiologist of the state board of health, visited the Level Green negro school, in Marlboro county, recently and made an announcement with regard to vaccination against smallpox, he says the pupils fled through doors and windows in terror and some time elapsed before they could be induced to return. About 100 pupils were vaccinated later at this school. In Marlboro county, some six or eight miles from Bennettsville, about 45 cases of smallpox have been located, none of which have been attended by a physician. Dr. Hayden says.

Dr. Hayden has returned to Colum-

"Students ran from smallpox vaccine in Marlboro"

Newspapers.com, Cheraw Chronicle, April 14, 1921, https://www.newspapers.com/article/cheraw-chronicle-students-ran-from-small/137051204/

Cheraw Gazette
Wed. Nov. 26, 1838 - Page 1

SALE OF NEGROES.

WILL be sold at Darlington Court House, on the first Monday in January, between

30 and 40 Negroes

nearly all of them able bodied men and women. These negroes belong to the estate of E. R. McIver and have been at work for some time on a Rail Road in Alabama.

Terms Cash.

JOHN K. McIVER, } Executors.
WM. C. McIVER, } E. R. McIver.

Nov. 25th, 1838.

Cheraw Gazette
Wed. Mar 27, 1839 - Page 3

Five Hundred Dollars Reward.

RANAWAY from my plantation, about a month since, my two negro men, Paul and Charles. From what I have recently learnt, I have no doubt they are harboured on some plantations on the river between this place and Society Hill. For proof to conviction of their being harboured by a white person I will give the above reward of Five Hundred Dollars; or I will give half that sum for proof to conviction of their being harboured by negroes. Or I will give One Hundred Dollars for their apprehension and lodgment in Chesterfield Jail or Fifty Dollars for either.

A. P. LACOSTE.

March 27, 1839.

Office Feb. 7, 1-40

Committed.

TO the Jail of Chesterfield District, on 25th inst. a negro woman who says belongs to ——— Goodwin of Richmond county N. C. and says that her name is Courtney that she is sometimes called, Mitilda. Said woman is about 25 years of age; about 4½ high and thick set. The owner is requested come forward prove property, pay charges, take her away.

O. GULLEDGE, Jailor

Chesterfield C. H. Feb. 26, 1840.

26

Sad Times

---

rs—Coffee—Tea—Bagging—Iron—ne—Mackarel—Soap—Candles—hot—Domestics—Flannels—Negro ckery—Glass Ware—Wines, &c.

2 improved lots in the town of C welling house thereon.

dry articles of Household Furnitur Sulkey and Harness

—ALSO—

r negroes, house servants will be al previously disposed of at Private Sa sale to continue from day to day u e sold.

Sale.

BY Permission of the Ordinary of Marlborough District, I will offer for sale, Wednesday the 11th day of March next, at the Market House in Cheraw, a likely negro fellow named Bill, belonging to the Estate of Hector McKinnon deceased. Bill is known to many of the boat owners on the river, as a valuable coxswain, and in all respects, a first rate negro. He is sold to pay the debts of the estate and not for any fault. Sale to take place at 12 o'clock A. Terms, one half cash; balance, 1st January next interest from day of sale, purchaser giving no with approved security. J. E. DAVID. Admr.

February 26, 1840. 16 2t

Historical Funny Times
Kicked out of church

Because four young women in his congregation giggled right out in meeting, Rev. George Robertson, pastor of a negro church has hailed them into police court on a charge of breaking up a church service. The magistrate continued the case until he could consult law and precedents on giggling.

Father of 47 Children

Daddy of Forty-seven.

New Bern.—A. S. Shields, a negro preacher who is the father of 47 children, celebrated his 72nd birthday with a fair gathering of his children around him. All but five of his children are living. He married a second time 18 years ago and has had 17 children by this marriage. Shields was a slave in the family of which Representative Claude Kitchin and former Governor W. W. Kitchin are members. He preaches his sermons in a church he owns himself.

Father of 32

GEORGIA NEGRO FATHER OF 32

Run Out of Names and Last Three Select Own as They Enter Public School.

Savannah, Ga.—A. B. Burgess, a negro employed by the Atlantic Coast Line railway, probably has the largest family in Georgia. He is the father of 32 children and has had three wives. Twenty-six of the children are living.

The negro has been blessed with seven sets of twins and two sets of triplets.

When the last set of twins were born, Burgess and his wife had run out of names for them and they went nameless until they selected their own names when they entered public school.

Burgess shied at selecting names when he found that among his progeny he had been "doubling up," having two "Willies" and two "Sallies" in his flock.

Cheraw Chronicle

Cheraw, South Carolina • Thu, Nov 3, 1921 Page 6

Not the Pee Dee area, but too funny not to

A Divorce at Age of 91.

Chicago.—Ambrose J. Rose, granted a decree of divorce from his third wife, asserted that "women were getting worse with every generation."

"My first wife was pretty good," he said, "my second was just medium and the third is no good at all." He asserted that he is through with them all."

Just want the dog

The Courier Waterloo, Iowa · Monday, May 10, 1954

HUSBAND AND DOG GONE; JUST WANTS DOG BACK

DALLAS, Tex. (AP)—A woman reported to police that her husband had disappeared with her Chihuahua puppy.

"I don't care if my husband ever comes back," she explained.

"I just want to find my dog."

Cheraw Chronicle Thu, Jul 28, 1921 ·Page

Man-Child on the Field
LaTonya Gordon with sons

There comes a time in every mother's life when she sees the man child she has raised or is raising and thinks oh how handsome he is. As a football mother my heart fills with pride as I watch those familiar numbers sprint onto the field for those endless plays. Your mouth says you cheer for the team. Your heart says you cheer for that man child you are raising. You say, "Make that tackle, catch that interception, block that pass."

Your life is hurried with sloppy meals during the season. You shuttle from workouts, practices, jamborees and games. You scope out the competition on the opposing team to see which one is going against your boy. You secretly pray for your man child to knock the wind out of him. You smile when he does.

Raising a household of football players there are always jerseys to wash for rec ball, cleats and mouth guards to buy. There is always a disarray of football socks. All of those things are to be expected; but I had a surreal moment not so long ago. This particular season I had a son playing recreational, one playing middle school, and a senior playing his last year.

On one of those hurried days I watched my middle school man child emerge from the locker room. He too was on his way to the big varsity game that was about to start. I nodded at him. He gave me a sly smile. The day before he had played one of the best games of the season. I watched as he eased into the bleachers with his teammates. I felt a slight twinge on my heartstrings. He no longer needed me.

My youngest lined up with his recreational team. They lined the field opposite the cheerleaders to welcome the varsity players. My man child was in the mist adorned in his suit of armor. Time seems to stand still. I nervously glanced up at my middle school son. He gave me that sly smile.

The varsity players erupted on the field, chanting, slapping the hands of cheerleaders and recreational players. I was in awe of the spirited show of comradery. My oldest slapped the hand of my youngest. They both stood in their jerseys watching each other. They glanced in the stands at my middle school son. It was at that moment I noticed all three had given that same sly smile. Not only did all three share the brotherhood of bloodline, but also through the boundaries of football. All three were connected by the former pig skinned prolate spheroid we called football. Today was a great week for all of my sons. This was a great day just to be their mother. I was disheartened because one was starting his football journey, one was still reaching his greatest potential, and one's journey was ending. This would be the last day they were all connected by football in such a way.

We won the game. When I was alone, I grieved inside because I knew I would never have them all that way again.

Walking With My Protector with
LaTonya Gordon with Mary Michelle Locke

It was a hot August night. The heat intensified as I walked on the hot asphalt. It was so dark I could barely see my cousin, Michelle who was a few steps ahead of me. I almost had to run to keep up with her. The only assurance that I had of her presence was the sound of her feet hitting the pavement. My pace of half running and half walking was beginning to make me sweat. My shirt was beginning to stick to my back from the extreme heat.

"Chelle, wait for me," I begged.

"You better walk up!" She snapped, annoyed that she had to walk me home, once again. My dad had called and said he was home from work and I could come home now. That meant Michelle had to be the one to walk me. I did not want her to walk me home any more than she wanted to walk me home, but our grandmother was determined that I was too young to walk home alone. We were stuck and had to get over our own issues. She was almost five years older than I was and she did not have time to deal with a little kid like me. I was still trying to figure out what was so great about being fifteen; you spend the whole year waiting to be sixteen.

We turned the curb closer to my house. Michelle was shadow boxing the air and dancing like Rocky. I didn't know if I should laugh or run. Sometimes she was funny and made me laugh. Other times she threatened to beat me up; unfortunately for me sometimes she did beat me up. That night I did not do anything, I kept walking until we were almost to my house. If I had to make a break for it and run from her I did not have far to go. Grandma would just have to deal with us later.

For some reason Michelle stopped doing her boxer impersonation and was looking towards my house. I looked at her a little dumbfounded for a minute. I was thinking this girl is up to something. This week her new trick was catching me off guard and scaring the mess out of me. I did not want any parts of that so I was watching her carefully waiting to see what she was going to do. This time she looked scared.

"What!" I asked.

"Shh!" She hissed.

"What do you see?" I asked her.

"Shut up stupid!" she fussed at me.

"No!" I snapped "What do you see?" I knew I was pushing my luck, but I wanted to know what scared someone who never got scared.

"There is a man behind your house!" She told me finally. We were too far away to see who the man was or what he was doing. All we could see was the figure of a man at the back of the house.

Fear and bravery billed up in my stomach, made it way up my throat and spilled out as words from my lips. "Hey," I shouted, "Who is that?"

Michelle grabbed my arm like I was protecting her. She tried to cover my mouth but it was too dark and she could not see. She missed my mouth and covered my nose. I was not satisfied the man never answered me. If he was going to hover around my house at least he could tell me his name.

"Who are you?" I was screaming now.

"Shut up fool!" My cousin demanded.

I ignored her; I wasn't going to run away from my own house. No stranger was going to make me leave when I was so close to home. That stranger did something I was not expecting to see. He stooped down next to the ground. He picked up a brick and started to run towards us.

Michelle, my protector, let go of my arm and took off running. I stood there for a minute then realized that a strange man was running towards me with a brick in his hand and my cousin was half way down the street in the wrong direction. My common sense kicked in, and I remembered that I was supposed to scream and I did it out loud. I turned away and ran to the front of my house and banged on my front door. I hollered for my daddy to open the door. He did not come. I screamed some more, and beat even louder. I did not see Michelle at all.

Someone called my name. I heard it between the screaming and the banging on the door. Someone called my name again. I looked up to see my father running up from beside the house. In his hand was a brick. I leaned into the door, looking at my dad, looking at the brick and looking at the road.

"I was fixing the cable wire," he started to laugh. "I saw you two coming up here and you were scared. I thought I would teach you a lesson about talking to strangers."

172

I didn't know if I should hit him or hug him. I was glad that the stranger turned out to be my dad. After a while of standing on the porch he scratched his head and asked, "What happened to Michelle?"

"She got scared and left me." I told him and laughed at the both of us.

"Well I guess she can't walk you home anymore." He laughed.

The next day at the bus stop, Michelle was waiting for me with a crazy look on her face. We both knew she was embarrassed that I saw how scared she was.

A note from the author

As a child, I had heard of the "two Marys" of the Bible, the beloved Mother of God, and the disreputable Mary Magdalen.   Naturally, I was taught to love the one who brought forth "The Great I Am". There were so many Christmas songs that were about her. The human side of me wanted to love the "Other Mary", the bad girl who turned good. Secretly I loved them both, but I often perked up at Pee Dee Union Baptist Church in South Carolina when "The Other Mary" was mentioned. I was intrigued by both of their lives. I did not know then that there would be two other women named Mary; who were connected to me that would plague my thoughts, rob me of hours of socializing, and much-needed sleep.

I believe I was born an amateur genealogist. I was always asking my parents questions about our relatives, looking at old pictures, and hearing my extended family tell our history. When I truly got an interest in genealogy I had to be honest with myself and ask a few questions: why was I doing it, what did I hope to gain, was I willing to share with others what I had learned, and how far did I want to go? I started first with one simple quest and that quest evolved. In the beginning, I wanted to find out about my maternal great-grandmother Mary. She passed away when my grandmother was only thirteen years old. There were no pictures or stories. I wanted to find Mary, to tell her story and her truth.

One July afternoon I was wondering if it was fair to only tell one story about one Mary in my tree. At that point in my research, there were thirty-one Marys connected to my family tree. My Biblical teaching made me think about Proverbs 31 and the virtuous woman. I refused to tell all the truths of my Marys. I knew my thoughts, these Marys were connected to me, I wasn't always thinking virtuously, so I was sure they weren't either. I also wanted to be able to go back home and have my family speak to me again. I liked the idea of not being told off, cussed out, or disowned because I told a story about one Mary that others felt I never should have told. Initially, I narrowed it down to just two women named Mary in my family tree. The first woman was Mary Sims, my maternal great-grandmother. The second was Mary Ann Quick, my paternal second great-grandmother.

The other Marys in my family tree lives also had value. These important loved ones shaped and educated those around them, but I chose the two that I knew the least about and the stories I wanted to tell. I didn't stop with the two of them, there were more stories to tell.

Grandmothers may their legacies continue

Although the novel is loosely based on facts references were needed and are listed below:

Abandoned Southeast. (2021, May 19). *Tuberculosis sanatorium*. Abandoned Southeast.
https://abandonedsoutheast.com/2020/02/15/tuberculosis-sanatorium/

"Adelaide Marshall Presenting Cab Calloway an Award" Newspapers.com, The Pittsburgh Courier, May 29, 1954, https://www.newspapers.com/article/the-pittsburgh-courier-adelaide-marshall/137708522/

Ancestry.com. *U.S., Federal Census Mortality Schedules, 1850-1885* [database on-line]. Lehi, UT, USA: Ancestry.com Operations, Inc., 2010. A portion of this collection was indexed by Ancestry World Archives Project contributors. Original data:

"Bernice Stokes Robinson." *South Carolina African American History Calendar*, 21 Jan. 2020, scafricanamerican.com/honorees/bernice-stokes-robinson/.

BDrakeford, Posted by BDrakeford   playing around with word press, & says:, M. N. J. (2016, May 30). *Collecting Family Fables – Mount Carmel Campgrounds*. Think   –   See   –   Do. https://brittneythenerd.com/2016/05/30/from-instagram-traveled-back-in-time-to-find-my-future-collecting-family-fables-blackfables-wp/

https://scafricanamerican.com/honorees/bernice-stokes-robinson/

Caldwell, A B. "Featured Collections." *Collections | HathiTrust Digital Library*, Digitized by Google from New Public Library, babel.hathitrust.org/cgi/mb. Accessed 03 May 2024.

Cheraw SC-South Carolina Ingram Hotel Court, vintage postcard. eBay. (n.d.). https://rb.gy/okunt

Cheraw Chronicle. (December 15, 1921). Mungo Brothers Arrested for Bootlegging. Newspapers.com. Retrieved July 21, 2023, from https://www.newspapers.com/article/cheraw-chronicle-mungo-brothers-arrested/128638252/

"Corona East Elmhurst Historic Preservation Society, Inc." *Lorraine Willis Gillespie, Was the Wife of Jazz Legend John Birks "Dizzy" Gillespie,* Ceehps.Org, www.facebook.com/CEEHPS/photos/a.1505165953104882/2894039817550815/?type=3. Accessed 27 Apr. 2024.

The Concord Daily Tribune. (March 22, 1919). Jacob Gordon Superintent of Church or Sunday School. Newspapers.com. Retrieved July 21, 2023, from https://www.newspapers.com/article/the-concord-daily-tribune-jacob-gordons/22038944/

"Dizzy Gillespie." *Dizzy Gillespie Happy 62nd Birthday to Jeanie Bryson,* Facebook, 10 Mar. 2020, www.facebook.com/DizzyGillespieJazz/photos/a.659250897437479/3166167330079144/?type=3. Accessed 27 Apr. 2024.

Documenting the American South: Oral histories of the American South. (n.d.). https://docsouth.unc.edu/sohp/G-0056-2/excerpts/excerpt_6211.html#fulltext

"FamilySearch.Org." *Family Search*, The Latter Day Saints of Jesus Christ, www.familysearch.org/ark:/61903/3:1: Accessed 5 Feb. 2024.

Florence Morning News, November 21, 1971, Page 1. via Newspapers.com (https://www.newspapers.com/article/florence-morning-news-mccall-twins-flo re/137051855/ : accessed May 6, 2024), clip page for McCall Twins Florence SC by user Ebonysky

"[Estates, Wills & Letters of Administration, 1791-1895; Index, 1791-1905; Author: Darlington County (South Carolina). Judge of Prob]," database with images, *Ancestry.com*([https://www.ancestry.com/discoveryui-content/view/1685610:9080?ssrc=pt &tid=27594265&pid=112297130276]: accessed [30 Jun 2023]), [Lucy Bostic].

Geiger, F. (1965) *The State 29 Nov 1965, page 22, Historical Newspapers from 1700s-2000s - Newspapers.com.* Available at: https://www.newspapers.com/image/749572580/?match=1&clipping_id=135964604 (Accessed: 29 November 2023).

Gibson , J. (2015) *Atlantic Beach: Historic African-american enclave in South Carolina: National Trust for Historic Preservation, Atlantic Beach: Historic African-American Enclave in South Carolina | National Trust for Historic Preservation.* Available at: https://savingplaces.org/stories/atlantic-beach-historic-african-american-enclave-in-south-c arolina (Accessed: 02 December 2023).

Gilbert, Shirly. "Slaves of William Hubbard, Marlboro County, South Carolina." *WikiTree*, INTERESTING.COM, INC, 2008, www.wikitree.com/wiki/Space:Slaves_of_William_Hubbard%2C_Marlboro_County%2C_South_Carolina.

Flemming-McCall, F. (2008). African Americans of Chesterfield County [Hardcover]. September 24, 2008.

Freeport Daily Bulletin 20 Oct 1904, page 2. Historical Newspapers from 1700s-2000s - Newspapers.com. (n.d.). https://www.newspapers.com/image/792805115/?clipping_id=130088409&fcfToken=ey JhbGciOiJIUzI1NiIsInR5cCI6IkpXVCJ9.eyJmcmVlLXZpZXctaWQiOjc5MjgwNTExN SwiaWF0IjoxNjk1MTYxMjAwLCJleHAiOjE2OTUyNDc2MDB9.1-Ud11G-eUrx9RHS 2iMpljXmYdH_jdPIjugXxvmXV-A

Florence Morning News. (October 26, 1926). G H Turner killed by black driver, hit and run. Newspapers.com. Retrieved July 21, 2023, from https://www.newspapers.com/article/florence-morning-news-g-h-turner-killed/54619896/

G. JACE. "A Bass Photo Album." *Classical Music Forum*, Talk Classical, 27 Sept. 2016, www.talkclassical.com/threads/a-bass-photo-album.40649/page-4.

Here Today, gone Tomorrow in Cheraw, SC. and Chesterfield County and surrounding areas. J & K Grill and Market, 99 Powe Street: late 2013. (n.d.). http://www.cherawclosings.com/2019/07/13/0/

The History of Atlantic Beach (no date) *Atlantic Beach, South Carolina - 'The black pearl'.* Available at: https://www.townofatlanticbeachsc.com/page/history (Accessed: 27 August 2023).

"History of Lancaster." *Lancaster South Carolina*, CrossPointe Studios, 2017, www.lancastercitysc.com/history-of-lancaster/#:~:text=The%20Lancaster%20area%20was %2C%20in,Catawba%2C%20and%20the%20Waxhaw%20tribes.

Historians of MSCC, Marlboro School Community Center, marlboroschoolcommunitycenter.org/mscc-history. Accessed 19 Jan. 2024.

""Husband and dog gone; just wants dog back"" Newspapers.com, The Courier, May 10, 1954,
https://www.newspapers.com/article/the-courier-husband-and-dog-gone-just/124384466/
Designed by NMP Information Service

"Lottie Gillespie" Newspapers.com, Transcript-Telegram, November 21, 1959,
https://www.newspapers.com/article/transcript-telegram-lottie-gillespie/146180882/

Make it Morris! (2021) *Morris College*. Available at: https://www.morris.edu/ (Accessed: 13 December 2023).

Maple, J.R. and Maples, D. (2014) *Wilson Maples, WikiTree*. Available at: https://www.wikitree.com/genealogy/MAPLES (Accessed: 06 March 2024).

Townships in Chesterfield County

"Marlboro County Museum." *Www.facebook.com*, 12 Feb. 2024 www.facebook.com/photo/?fbid=827891106002332&set=a.477858734338906. Accessed 21 May 2024. Rev. Arthur J. Wright with wife Maggie Bowen Wright

McCall, Spencer. "Cousin Attorney John E. McCall SC Lawyers Meeting." *Facebook*, 18 Jan. 2023, m.facebook.com/photo.php?photo_id=163951643055624.

Mt. Carmel Campground Historical Marker. Historical Marker. (2023, September 4). https://www.hmdb.org/m.asp?m=23915

The Nation's Most Renowned Pee Dee Choral Ensemble, Cheraw, South Carolina, Baylor University,
digitalcollections-baylor.quartexcollections.com/Documents/Detail/the-nations-most-renowned-pee-dee-choral-ensemble-cheraw-south-carolina/1877954?item=1877957. Accessed 30 Dec. 2023.

New Hopewell Baptist Church (2022) *Facebook*. Available at: https://www.facebook.com/photo.php?fbid=172071288789020&set=pb.100079584481499.-2207520000&type=3 (Accessed: 13 December 2023).

Newspapers.com, The Journal News, January 6, 2000, https://www.newspapers.com/article/the-journal-news/146187138/

Online publication - Provo, UT, USA: Ancestry.com Operations Inc, 2008.Original data - South Carolina. South Carolina death records. Columbia, SC, USA: South Carolina Department of Archives and History.Original data: South Carolina. South Carolina death re

"Our History." *Columbia Hospital School of Nursing Alumnae Association CHSNAA*, Columbia Hospital School of Nursing Alumnae Association, chsnaa.org/class-pictures/. Accessed 10 Dec. 2023.

"Our Office." *Ingram Law Firm*, Ingram Law Firm, www.cherawlaw.com/office. Accessed 10 Dec. 2023.

"Race and Slavery Petitions, Digital Library on American Slavery." *Dlas.uncg.edu*, dlas.uncg.edu/petitions/petition/21386325/.

 Seaboard Coast LIne (Atlantic Coast Line) Railway Station Cheraw, S.C., University of South Carolina, 2008, digital.tcl.sc.edu/digital/collection/rrc/id/1504/rec/1.

"Students ran from smallpox vaccine in Marlboro" Newspapers.com, Cheraw Chronicle, April 14, 1921, https://www.newspapers.com/article/cheraw-chronicle-students-ran-from-small/137051204/

Smalls, B., Montgomery, J. and Hennigan, C. (2016) The History of Atlantic Beach, Atlantic Beach, South Carolina - 'The black pearl'. Available at: https://www.townofatlanticbeachsc.com/page/history (Accessed: 27 August 2023).

J and K grill and market. Foursquare. (n.d.). https://rb.gy/lmtg3

The item 26 Sep 1924, page 4 (1924) *Historical Newspapers from 1700s-2000s - Newspapers.com.* Available at: https://www.newspapers.com/image/668736430/?match=1 (Accessed: 28 November 2023).

The State (Columbia, South Carolina) · 10 Sep 1942, Thu · Page 16

Green, Victor. "The Negro Motorist Green Book." Wikipedia, Wikimedia Foundation, 18 Dec. 2023, en.wikipedia.org/wiki/The_Negro_Motorist_Green_Book.

"United States Census (Slave Schedule), 1850 ", database with images, *FamilySearch* (https://familysearch.org/ark:/61903/1:1:HRWZ-KV3Z : 23 February 2021), Benjamin Quick in entry for MM9.1.1/MV8M-QP6:, 1850.
"United States Census (Slave Schedule), 1860", database with images, *FamilySearch* (https://www.familysearch.org/ark:/61903/1:1:WKR3-Z16Z : Tue Jul 11 16:41:33 UTC 2023), Entry for Geo R Boatwright and , 1860.

"United States Census (Slave Schedule), 1850 ", database with images, *FamilySearch* (https://familysearch.org/ark:/61903/1:1:HRWZ-KNMM : 15 March 2022), J W Harrington in entry for MM9.1.1/MV8M-Q1L:, 1850.

"United States Census (Slave Schedule), 1860", database with images, *FamilySearch* (https://www.familysearch.org/ark:/61903/1:1:WKR8-BB2M : Thu Jun 15 19:58:28 UTC 2023), Entry for O H Kollock and , 1860.

Walton-Raji, Angela Y. "Remembering the Old Schools - the Pillars of Our Communities." *Remembering the Old Schools - the Pillars of Our Communities*, Blogspot, Oct. 2011,

myancestorsname.blogspot.com/2010/11/remembering-old-schools-pilars-of-o
ur.html.

Weston, Z. (1997) *The item 12 Oct 1997, page 23, Historical Newspapers from 1700s-2000s - Newspapers.com*. Available at: https://www.newspapers.com/image/669465089/?terms=LaTonya+Gordo n&match=1&clipping_id=116082199 (Accessed: 28 November 2023).

"Women acting up in church" Newspapers.com, Cheraw Chronicle, June 29, 1922, https://basic.newspapers.com/article/cheraw-chronicle-women-acting-up-i n-chur/25141572/

Check out these other titles by the author

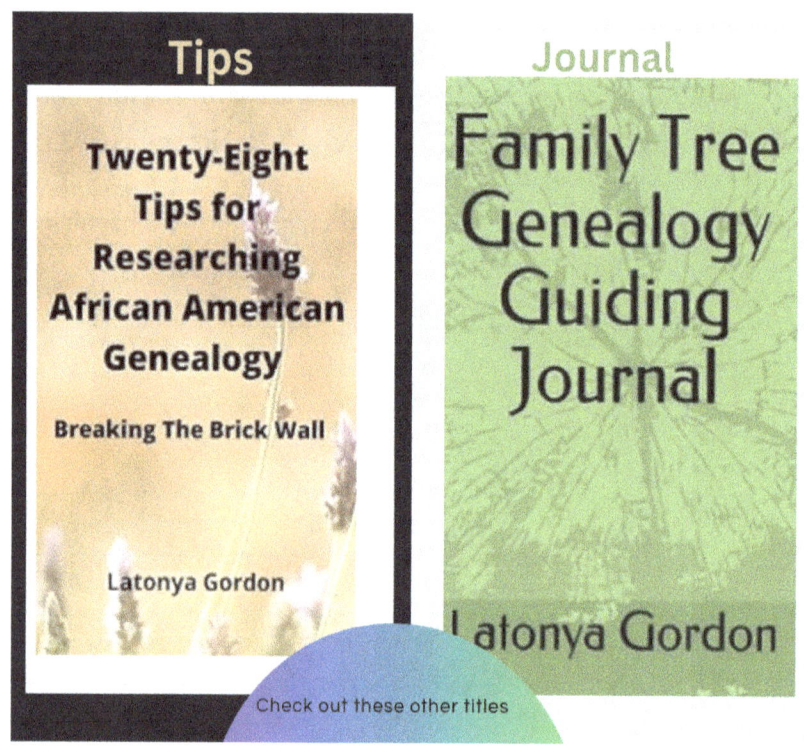